Hold Fast to Dreams

Hold Fast to
DREAMS

ANDREA DAVIS PINKNEY

HYPERION PAPERBACKS FOR CHILDREN
NEW YORK

Excerpts from the poems "Dreams" and "Youth," as
quoted on pages 103 and 104,
are from *The Dreamkeeper and Other Poems*, by Langston Hughes,
copyright 1932 by Alfred A. Knopf, Incorporated, and renewed 1960 by Langston Hughes.
Reprinted by permission of his publisher.

First Hyperion Paperback edition 1996

Text ©1995 by Andrea Davis Pinkney.
First published in hardcover in 1995.
Reprinted by permission of William Morrow and Company, Inc.

1 3 5 7 9 10 8 6 4 2

The text for this book is set in 12-point Caledonia.

Library of Congress Cataloging-in-Publication Data

Pinkney, Andrea Davis.
Hold fast to dreams / Andrea Davis Pinkney. — 1st Hyperion
Paperback ed.
p.   cm.
Summary: Twelve-year-old Deirdre, whose passion for photography
has earned her the nickname "Camera Dee," feels uncomfortable being
the only black student at her new school.
ISBN 0-7868-1125-0
[1. Moving, Household—Fiction. 2. Prejudices—Fiction.
3. Photography—Fiction. 4. Afro-Americans—Fiction.] I. Title.
[PZ7.P6333Ho   1996]
[Fic]—dc20   96-1985

No other black kids? That couldn't be right. But my friend Lorelle, she said she knew the deal: In places like Wexford, everybody's white. Yeah, Lorelle, she told me. No wonder I couldn't sleep. And that *dream*—no way was I gonna stay in bed for more of that.

I made it to the bottom of the staircase and tiptoed through the front hall, trying to figure out how to walk around our new house in the dark without making noise, without waking up Dad or Lindsay—or Mom, who hears everything.

Moving boxes cluttered the kitchen, and that tile floor was *freezing*.

Mom hadn't hung any curtains yet, so the half-circle moon glowed into the kitchen, casting a creamy haze over the room. Luckily, I could make out the refrigerator. I opened its door, praying the hinges wouldn't creak too loudly. Light splashed out onto my face and spread to the bare walls around me. I squinted and rubbed my eyes.

We had moved into our house only that morning, but our

refrigerator was already full of food. Mom could always find the nearest grocery store, and she didn't waste time stocking up on enough to feed us for at least three weeks.

I slid two slices of rye bread from their cellophane bag. Then I remembered: No one had unpacked the silverware, so I couldn't get a knife to spread mayonnaise or slice cheese for a sandwich. I couldn't even grab a spoon to stir up some chocolate milk. What a pain. Who wanted food, anyway? I knew that if I ate, I'd probably get all full, then go back upstairs and sink into another nightmare.

I wedged a small moving carton into the refrigerator's open door to keep the light on. I couldn't flick on the stronger overhead light. Mom and Dad's bedroom was right off the top of the stairs, and it would wake up Mom for sure, since she was such a light sleeper.

Finding a bigger box to sit on, I looked around the empty room. What *would* this new school be like? Maybe Lorelle had made a mistake. Lorelle, my best friend—my *girl*—in Baltimore, told me I could count on one hand the black families who lived in towns like Wexford, Connecticut. She said the people in Wexford wouldn't be used to black folks and would give me a hard time because I'm black and smart—too smart, sometimes, is what Lorelle used to say. Thinking about what Lorelle had told me about places like Wexford gave me one of those woozy chills, all over my body.

I hugged myself to keep from shivering. I figured Lindsay would have an easy time of it. She'd make sure they treated her right at that private school. Lindsay didn't take stuff from nobody. Now that Mom and Dad had the money, they kept bugging me about going to Green Crest with Lindsay. But who wanted to end up at some snobby prep school? Besides, Lorelle told me white kids would treat me even meaner there. She said her cousin went to a prep school and got messed with.

A noisy wind blew outside, announcing the beginning of spring. I tried to remember if I'd ever heard the wind blowing at night in Baltimore. Maybe an occasional siren or somebody walking by our building, playing his music, but never any wind. I listened for that wind again. Instead, I heard creaking foot-steps in the hall.

"I thought we had a burglar." Mom leaned in the kitchen doorway, wearing her bathrobe. My shoulders jumped; Mom had startled me. "It wouldn't matter, anyway," Mom said. "There's not much here to steal, unless we had a hungry bur-glar who wanted to raid the fridge." The refrigerator's soft light showed off Mom's frame—a tall tawny lady with soul in her eyes is how my daddy always describes her.

Mom sat on a box next to mine. Her eyes seemed calm at first, but then I looked closer. In the refrigerator's light, I could see she was watching little worries that sprang up in front of her thoughts.

"And, miss, what are *you* doing sitting here at this ungodly hour—the middle of the night, before your first day at your new school?" she asked.

"I thought I was hungry, but I don't feel like eating. So I'm just sitting here thinking."

Mom smiled. "You were always a good thinker, Dee. You think more than any twelve-year-old I know."

"Yeah." I nodded and felt my lips make a little smile. Mom liked to praise me for my thinking.

"How about sharing some of your thoughts with me?" Mom asked. "I tossed and squirmed in bed, doing some think-ing myself," she said, "then your father started his buzz-saw snoring, so I got up to unpack a few of these boxes."

I hugged myself tighter. "Mom, I had an *awful* dream."

Mom pulled the lapels of her bathrobe closer together, causing her robe to tug at her shoulders, the shoulders I'm always asking God to let me inherit when I'm grown, even though I think Lindsay—tall and tone, like Mom—will get those broad shoulders, not me.

"I dreamt I lived in a place where at night the moon was black and the sky was white. The scariest part is that everyone else in the dream walked around like it was normal—a black moon surrounded by a white sky. The same backward black and white as the film negatives that come with my pictures." I was raising my voice, speaking a mile a minute.

Mom frowned. "Dee, honey, hush now. I'm here; it's all right. Try to forget about it."

"*No*. Let me *finish*." I wanted to tell it all, get rid of it. My butt was starting to go numb on the flat cardboard box. "Nobody else noticed that things were all reversed and messed up. Everywhere I went, I told people, 'This isn't what it's like where I come from. This isn't how things are supposed to be.' But nobody paid me no mind. It was like I was from another planet or something, like I had no business being in a turned-around place like that." I folded my arms.

Mom stroked my hair. She gently led my cheek to her soft, full bosom and held it there, safe.

"Dreams," she said. "Isn't it funny, Dee. We have so many dreams we pray will come true. And others we hope never come to pass—those dark dreams that wake you up and bother you for days afterward."

"My dream sure woke me up," I said, "and got me thinking about tomorrow, about my new school—full of white kids." I played with the ruffle on the sleeve of my nightgown. "Mom, I don't want to go to that school. Lorelle said there aren't any black families in Wexford. Is that for real?"

"I don't know, Dee, girl. And to be honest, I'm scared too. I lived in Baltimore most of my life. I don't know a thing about Wexford, Connecticut."

I think you know some things about Wexford that you don't want to come right out and say, I thought. *How could you not know anything about Wexford? You came with Dad to pick out our house. You had to be checking it out then.*

Mom's eyes roamed, restless. Maybe she didn't know about Wexford in her head, like when you ask somebody if they know the answer to a question. But I think Mom knew about Wexford in a place other than her head.

"Dee, there may *not* be many black kids at your school, but you get along with most people. Remember all those friends you had back home, kids coming over, sitting out on the front stoop, asking you to take their picture?" Mom hummed a little laugh. Her body loosened.

"Yeah, but those were *black* kids who hung on our stoop, my friends from school. I don't know if *most* people—white kids, I mean—will get along with *me*."

"Listen, Dee, you're going to meet all kinds of folks. You and Lindsay will have experiences your father and I never dreamed of."

"Like what?" I looked at Mom sideways. She didn't answer me right away. She was staring at her hands, curling them around each other.

After a moment, she confessed, "I don't know. We'll have to wait and see." I scooted closer to Mom, letting the refrigerator door swing shut. I didn't need the light anymore. The sound of Mom's voice was enough.

Mom sighed and put her arms around my shoulders, giving them a little squeeze. Then we sat there, not talking, staring into the dark.

* * *

The trees on the street wore the leaf buds of early spring. Their trunks outlined the corner of Mayflower Drive and Scarlet Oak Lane. I waited there for the school bus, drawing designs in the dirt underneath my shoes, remembering my bad dream from the night before. Scarlet Oak Lane, the street where our new house sat, seemed to stretch on forever with nothing more than grass, sky, and little birds that flew from tree to tree.

Connecticut didn't look anything like Redmond Avenue, our street in Baltimore. There, everybody I knew lived in apartment buildings. Lorelle and I walked to school, six blocks away.

The inside of my nose started to tickle and my eyes itched—the sensation they talk about on those hay fever commercials, where some lady's standing in a field of weeds, waving a white flag of surrender. I sneezed harder than ever, wishing for my own surrender flag.

Through sniffles, my thoughts turned to last summer's block party, where Lorelle and I organized a double-dutch team for the younger girls on Redmond Avenue and for some of the kids who lived on Carver Place, one block over. We called ourselves the Jumpin' Jive Five. And thanks to the double-dutch rhythms I made up and the jump rope combinations Lorelle worked out, we were the best jumpers around. Everyone said we could do some serious rope.

> We call ourselves the Jumpin' Jive Five.
> When we get down, the rope comes alive.
> Jumpin' over the moon. Jumpin' over the sun.
> Got two ropes twirlin' instead of one!

That rhyme played itself over and over in my head, accented by my sneezes. But when I sang "Jumpin' Jive Five" quietly to

myself, it didn't sound the same. How could it, with me standing alone—with hay fever? I wanted to jump the Jive Five jump,
but I couldn't, not on this strange street, with nobody around.

Scarlet Oak Lane was wrong for jumping double-dutch. To
jump right, I needed street noises—car horns and city buses—
and the boys from our neighborhood passing by, talking trash.
I kicked a pebble. My head hurt, and thinking about Lorelle
sent a stony lump to my throat.

I stared up at the trees that towered overhead and felt the
strap of my camera pinch the back of my neck. Mom had told
me to leave my camera home, this being my first day. I told her
that if I was going to school, my camera was coming with me.
She didn't argue.

I looked through the camera's viewfinder up at the tree
limbs that decorated the cloudless sky. Before I could focus on
a shot, the rumble of the school bus's motor ruined my con-
centration. Slowly, the bus rolled into view, its motor revving
louder and louder. I sneezed again, and that hard thing in my
throat raced to my stomach.

"You new?" the driver asked me as I stepped onto the bus.

"Uh-huh. Yeah. New—Willis. My name is Deirdre Willis.
I'm new." I always trip up my talking when I'm scared. And it
didn't help much that the bus driver didn't look right. He had
one of those mustaches that curls around like a bandit's. Mom
says it's not nice to stare, so I tried not to watch him too close.
Instead, I looked at all those white kids *staring* at *me*. I walked
up the aisle of the bus to find a seat. Some students stopped
talking when I passed. A few of them whispered. My sneeziness
slipped away, but my heart pumped a silent, uneven rhythm inside my chest.

My blood flashed hot, sending clammy sweat to my palms
and armpits. I took the first empty seat I saw, slid close to the

bus window, and sat as still as a statue. The students around me spoke with each other, sending broken pieces of talk past my ears:

"...and what rhymes with *lacrosse?*"

"Dental floss."

"*Her?*...won't make the team...runs too slow—"

"...went to lacrosse camp to learn to play with the—"

"...tryouts until—"

I folded my arms and slouched in my seat, wishing I could shrivel up, disappear, then show up again on Lorelle's front stoop. I'd tell her how Wexford is no place for a Jumpin' Jive Fiver and how much I've missed her. "Yeah, you were right, Lorelle," I heard myself saying.

In that moment, somewhere between confusion and feeling low-down in the dumps, a tiny thought whispered to me: I've never been anyplace where I'm the *only* black person.

A frightened loneliness pounced on my shoulders. It wriggled down my back, wrapped its heavy arms around me, and held on tight.

2

"Look awake, will you please? This is Miss Deirdre Willis. She's just moved here from Maryland. I know you'll all welcome her." I stood at the front of my first-period class with Mr. McCurdy, the seventh-grade English teacher. Mr. McCurdy spoke with a voice like rusted shutters, and his wrinkled skin was pinker than a Sunday ham. He must have been a hundred years old, or older.

I leaned away when Mr. McCurdy spoke, partly because he seemed so evil, partly to get a better look at his craggy face. And while I eyeballed my new teacher, I noticed that the kids in my class were checking me out like nobody's business. At first, I thought they were only gawking at my camera, but their eyes moved from my hair to my sweater, down to my shoes, then back and forth at each other.

I shrugged and swallowed and didn't look at any of them, my heart still pounding like bongos in a band.

"Miss Willis, there's your seat, over there. Take it, won't you please." Mr. McCurdy pointed to an empty desk toward the front of the room. I sat down, cradling my camera in my lap. I carefully looked right, then left.

Mr. McCurdy rubbed his hands together. "Now listen up. Today we're starting our unit on great American poets. Who can name some?"

The other kids were slow to answer, so I raised my hand. When Mr. McCurdy called on me, I cleared my throat. That lump was still resting there from before. "Langston Hughes," I said softly.

"*Hughes*. L-a-n-g-s-t-o-n H-u-g-h-e-s." Mr. McCurdy wrote the poet's name on the blackboard.

"Langston *who*?" asked a red-haired girl sitting next to me.

I thought everybody knew who Langston Hughes was. Langston *who*? She had her nerve. I sucked my teeth silently and folded my arms. Then I glanced around to get a better look at the red-haired girl. She wore a lopsided smirk and chomped on a wad of gum, even though the sign on the door said NO GUM, NO RADIOS, NO FOOD IN CLASS.

"Hughes. A fine poet. One of our best," Mr. McCurdy was saying. "Miss Willis, stand up, please, and expand on Langston Hughes." I pushed my glasses up on my nose and stood up.

"Well, sure," I said, watching the red-haired girl out of the corner of my eye. "Langston Hughes was an African-American poet who got popular in the 1920s and 1930s. He wrote plays and essays, too." I spoke slowly and carefully. My fidgety heart started to beat regularly again.

"And Langston Hughes helped shape what is known as the Harlem Renaissance," Mr. McCurdy explained.

"He spent a year in Mexico with his father after he was done with high school," I added.

"Born in Joplin, Missouri," Mr. McCurdy said.

"His poem 'The Weary Blues' won him a prize." Mr. McCurdy and I, we were on a roll.

"*The Weary Blues* turned out to be the title of Hughes's first book of poems, published in 1926," he said.

I'd never had a teacher go on with me like that. Mr. McCurdy, crusty and old as he was, knew a lot about Langston Hughes. He looked pleased that I knew almost as much as he did. In his broken-hinge voice, he said, "That'll be all for now. Your seat, Miss Willis. You may take it."

Everybody got quiet; I guess they were waiting for me to sit down. But I didn't want to take my seat; I didn't want to take *any* seat. I was just getting started. Those kids were still staring, still checking me out. I wanted to tell them more about Langston Hughes, and about the other African-American poets who are my favorites—like Gwendolyn Brooks and Nikki Giovanni. I was willing to bet my camera that none of those white kids had heard of *them*.

The red-haired girl had stopped smirking. She was paying attention, listening to me and Mr. McCurdy talk about Langston Hughes. I don't think she knew what to make of me. When I caught her staring, her eyes snapped to her lap.

Before I sat back down, I spotted a folded sheet of paper on my seat. I eased into my chair and opened the paper, holding it beneath my desk so nobody else could see. The note said:

> *Langston Hughes sounds cool. I'd like to know more about him, and more about you, too. Later.*
>
> *—Web*
>
> *P.S. McCurdy's old as mold, so watch out.*

I glanced around the classroom to see who'd left the note. But nobody nodded or looked my way or anything. So I shoved the note in my knapsack, curious and a little excited. That note couldn't have come from a boy, because the handwriting was too neat. But who could've belonged to a name like Web?

When the bell rang, I let out a breath and gathered my books. The other students huddled together in groups of twos and threes, leaving me alone in the classroom with Mr. McCurdy.

"You've got a fire for good poets, I can see that," he said, clasping my hand with a two-handed handshake. I gently pulled my hand free and adjusted my knapsack.

Mr. McCurdy gestured toward my camera. "Maybe someday you'll show us all how you use that thing," he said.

"Maybe." I tried to smile. But when I looked up, I noticed Mr. McCurdy's jagged, nasty teeth and the hairs that grew out from his nostrils. I won't be taking *your* picture, I thought. Mr. McCurdy nodded. "Very good, then," he said.

As he left, the door brushed closed quietly behind him. I looked back at the empty classroom.

That evening, Mom and Lindsay and I made dinner. "So how was it, you two?" Mom asked. "I want to hear all about your first day, so I can tell your father when he gets home. He's working late tonight, trying to impress them already."

I stood at the sink, scrubbing potatoes with a vegetable brush, while Lindsay peeled carrots for a salad. "Green Crest beats Rosa Parks Public any day! Some of the girls are snobby, but I don't care about them." Excited as she was, Lindsay spoke with hardly a breath between her sentences. "I signed up for girls' lacrosse tryouts next week. It seems like a stupid game, but I'll figure out how to play it somehow," she said. I thought about Mr. McCurdy's class and my ride on the school bus— and all that talk about lacrosse.

"There aren't any black kids at Green Crest," Lindsay said. "Well, there's one. I think his name is Barry or Larry, something like that. Anyway, I think he's in fifth grade, so I won't really see him much around us sixth graders. Larry—or Barry—doesn't live in Connecticut, though. He's from New York City and goes to Green Crest on a scholarship." Lindsay had eyes just like Mom's, round and bright, like agate stones. For her first day of school, she clipped her dress-up barrettes to the end of her braids. Her thick, pretty hair outlined her cheeks.

Mom fumbled through the cupboards, looking for something to add to the pot of cabbage that was simmering on the stove. "Larry," she said, giving Lindsay half her attention, "did you speak to him at all?"

"Nah. But I talked to some of the other kids. A lot of them seemed decent. But one girl asked me if I was there as part of some kind of special inner-city *minority* program."

Mom put her fingertips to her lips; she couldn't find what she was looking for. "Minority program? What did you tell her?" she asked. Mom could carry on a conversation and make dinner at the same time. But I never tried to tell her something important while she cooked. I'd wait till later, when she could really listen.

I scrubbed and scrubbed the skin on the potatoes while Lindsay did most of the talking.

"I told her *no*. That I'm not some special minority." Lindsay snatched leaves from a head of lettuce, ripping them into little pieces. "Anyway, I said I'd just moved here from Baltimore. And that we live in Wexford now. It's no big deal, but sometimes you have to explain *everything* to white folks."

"What did you do when they looked at you strange?" I asked.

"I looked at *them* strange," Lindsay said.

Mom handed Lindsay a stack of plates. She gestured with her chin, signaling Lindsay to set the table. At each place setting, Lindsay made sloppy napkin folds and paid no mind to the forks she placed upside down. "Lord, give me patience," Mom whispered.

"Huh, Mom, what'd you say?" Lindsay asked.

"Don't mind me, Linds," Mom said, "I'm just talking to myself. I said, 'Lord, this kitchen is *spacious.*'" Mom winked at me.

"Dee, how was your day?" she asked, closing the oven door on baked chicken parts.

"My day?" The faucet water turned from warm to hot. I dropped a potato in the sink, sucked in a breath, and turned on the cold water. "Wexford Middle School was cool by me," I said. "Everyone asked me all kinds of questions about Baltimore. Some kids even wanted me to take their picture." I knew Mom knew I was lying, because she didn't speak right away. She helped Lindsay finish setting the table.

"Sounds like you made some new friends," Mom said.

"A few," I answered, quick and quiet.

After dinner, Lindsay slipped away from helping with cleanup. Green Crest gave out lots of homework, she said.

I knelt and tilted the dustpan while Mom swept the last crumbs of dirt off the kitchen floor. I watched Mom's feet do a swift little dance. Mom had played girls' basketball when she was my age, and her coordination showed it. Her size-ten feet (I never wanted to inherit those) swept the floor as easy as the broom, her sneakers making soft skids on the tile.

"Mom, Wexford Middle School *wasn't* all cool by me. Some stuff was cool, but there's other stuff about that place that made me want to not go back—ever," I said.

"I could see you weren't telling the whole truth. Lord knows, Dee, girl. If I haven't taught you anything else, I hope I've taught you to be honest." A tiny sting of shame twinged inside me. Mom put the broom away in the kitchen closet, then wiped down the refrigerator door.

"I *am* honest—most of the time." I couldn't look at Mom, at least not in her eyes. So I peered out the kitchen window at a squirrel who ran back and forth on the same branch, confused about which way to scoot.

"I know one thing," Mom said. "When you have a good day, you don't let your sister talk so much. For a girl who's just turned eleven, she can keep any conversation going. But Deirdre, I've seen you match her."

Mom spooned cherry Jell-O—my favorite—into a small bowl. She topped the jiggly dessert with a little plop of whipped cream and brought the bowl to the kitchen table, where I sat.

"Mom, why *did* we move here, anyway? I liked Baltimore better. The kids aren't friendly here. And the only black face I saw at school was my own, when I looked at the mirror in the girls' room.

"I couldn't have a conversation with people—a *real* conversation, I mean. On the school bus, everybody talked about some game called lacrosse, that thing Lindsay said she's gonna try out for. I don't think anyone jumps double-dutch here, or even plays hopscotch." I slurped some Jell-O.

"And it gets worse!" I sucked my teeth and sniffled back a runny nose. Those hay fever sneezes were kicking up again. "In class, we started a unit on American poets. Do you believe nobody had ever heard of Langston Hughes? Well, nobody except my teacher, Mr. McCurdy. But Mom, Mr. McCurdy's this wrinkly old man. The way his body hunches over, he looks like a candy cane with feet. And his shoes, they're the color of stewed prunes. Talks like a train engine too. *Scary!*"

Mom took a napkin from the holder on the table and gently tucked it into my palm. I wiped my nose.

"Sweetheart, this was your first day. Give it time. We moved here because your father wants us to have the best."

"*Baltimore* was the best!" I said.

Mom got up to dip herself a bowl of Jell-O from the refrigerator. Then she sat back down, next to me.

"Dee, your father and I love you," she said. I shrugged and played with my whipped cream.

"Mom, I *know*. I know you both *love* me. I just want—"

"Listen, Dee. Please. Let me speak for a moment." Mom leaned forward and pressed on my arm to hush me. She looked serious; she spoke low.

"I've known your father since I was younger than you are now." Oh no, I thought, here it comes, the story I've heard a billion trillion times. I huffed out loud.

"When he was ten years old," Mom went on, "he got a paper route to earn money to buy his mother a washing machine so that she could stop wearing down the skin on her hands, scrubbing clothes in a metal basin. And so she could rest when she got home at night after cleaning white people's houses and caring for their children all day."

I knew this story by heart, the same way I knew the words to songs on the radio. I couldn't help but interrupt. "Yeah, yeah," I said, "in the coldest weather and in the blazing heat of August, Dad tossed those papers—every day, without fail—on porches all over the neighborhood."

Mom wouldn't let me finish. She gave me a stern look and picked up from there. "Everyone thought your father was crazy, because he wouldn't miss a day of delivering papers for anything. When all the kids asked him why he worked so hard, he'd say—"

I jumped in again before Mom could go ahead. "'Because I want the best for my mother. If I work hard, she won't have to.'"

I shifted in my chair and turned away from Mom. That squirrel had found a friend, a larger squirrel who showed her the way up the tree outside our kitchen window. I did my best to keep listening to Mom.

"Your father saved his money for months. It took him more than two years to sock away enough to buy the first rotary washing machine any black family had ever owned in Colesville, Virginia. When that washer was delivered, Gebba just couldn't stop smiling. She was so proud that her son had worked so hard to bring her a little bit of comfort." Mom's eyes narrowed at the memory. The tree outside stood empty. The squirrels had run off to play.

"After that, everyone treated your father differently; they gave him respect. The older boys let him play their games, and even white boys respected him. They still called the other black boys names, but not your father."

Mom loved to tell this story. The last time was when Daddy came home from work and told us he'd gotten the job at Kentwood, in New York City, and that we'd be moving to Connecticut. I tried to picture Dad as a little kid, selling newspapers. Most of the time, I couldn't imagine it. It was easy to picture Daddy working hard. Still, I couldn't help but roll my eyes.

"Mom, what does this story have to do with *me*? I have no friends in this 'for whites only' town!"

Mom's lips parted slightly, showing the small gap that separated her front teeth. "Listen, don't start with me, lady. And take your hand off your hip," she said. "Your father is seeing a dream he's wanted for a long time. And neither you nor I are going to stop him. He's worked his *tail* off so that you kids can have it better than we did. Don't you forget that—ever!" Mom's eyes stayed on me. She breathed heavily, then frowned.

I drew back. Cutting my eyes toward Mom, I noticed baggy hollows of skin hanging just under her lower eyelids. Maybe moving and the new house and all was making her moody. She probably missed Baltimore—where our kitchen was no more than a nook that smelled of collards—as much as I did. But all she talked about was what Dad wanted and how we all should want it too. It was as if she never stopped to think about what moving to Connecticut meant to *her*.

Still, I was the one who rode the school bus and sat in that classroom with that creaky teacher and those beady-eyed kids. And I was sick of trying to make Mom understand my side of it.

Before Mom could speak again, I stood up from the table and put my empty Jell-O bowl in the sink. I tossed my spoon in with it, its clatter adding to the anger that already swirled around the room.

Then I walked toward the staircase. Halfway up the stairs, I turned to Mom. "I can't tell you *anything* without getting some dumb lecture about being black and working hard. Did you ever stop to think about *me*? Just because Daddy's worked hard doesn't mean I'm supposed to like it here. I never wanted to move here in the first place! Maybe Wexford is the best—but for *who*? You? Dad? Lindsay?" I kicked the stair in front of me, then ran up to my bedroom as fast as I could.

3

Dad came home late from work—again. His new job had kept him at the office. All week he'd missed eating dinner with Mom, Lindsay, and me. Every night, Mom would keep his dinner warm in the oven, on a foil-covered plate. Then she'd sit with Dad at the kitchen table while he ate his dried-out meal.

Tonight, after Dad changed his clothes, he fell asleep on the couch without even making it to the kitchen. I could hear Mom setting up the TV tray table, so she could bring Dad's dinner to him in the family room.

Lindsay was upstairs, taking a shower. I sat on the carpet, loading film in my camera, my back resting against the arm of our sofa, where Dad slept. Dad's breathing was slow and heavy, and loud enough to hear. A bouquet of flowers stood in a vase on the end table next to the sofa. Dad had brought home red roses for Mom. I think he felt bad about missing dinner every night and somehow wanted to make it up to Mom.

Roses. Just like the ones Dad had come home with on that night a few months ago, when we still lived in Baltimore.

That night in our old house on Redmond Avenue must

have played in my mind a million times. Like every night, Dad had come home from the office at six, like clockwork. We were all used to his comings and goings. So when Dad's key unlocked the front door, Mom didn't even look up from her desk, where she sat grading papers, and Lindsay and I stayed sprawled out on the living room rug, marking pages in the Sears catalog, looking at stuff we wanted for Christmas.

Dad yanked off his tie and kissed Mom on the cheek with a loud smooch. Behind his back, he hid the flowers, roses with long, prickly stems. He was snapping his fingers and singing his favorite old song, the one about an easy walk in the sunshine. Dad squeezed Mom around the waist. He startled her into a giggly squeal, then teased the bouquet in front of her nose. "Come here, you fine thing, and smell *these*. They're sweet, like you. Sweet like life. *Sweet*," he said.

"Let me guess"—Mom sniffed the bouquet—"you won the lottery."

"Better," Dad said.

"Oh, no, they're getting all lovey-dovey again." Lindsay rolled her eyes.

I threw her a sideways look. "Get grown," I said. "Don't you know anything about romance?" Lindsay shrugged and kept flipping pages from the catalog.

"I bet you called the hot-line contest on the radio and won fifty-yard-line seats to the Redskins playoff game." That was my guess. Dad's smirk tugged at his mustache. He jiggled a rose loose from the bouquet, snapped off the stem, and tucked the flower behind his ear. "You're not even close."

Mom stacked her ungraded spelling tests. Her second graders would have to wait. "Bennett, this guessing game is crazier than you are. *Tell* us!" She searched the bouquet for a card, a clue.

"Yeah, Dad, don't leave us hanging like this," Lindsay said.

"Right," I said, "this is cruel and mean."

Mom carefully unwrapped her roses. She hurried to the kitchen to fill a vase with water. "Don't give any more hints until I come back," she said, waving a finger toward Dad.

At the stereo, Dad turned on the music. He started dancing before his song came on. When Mom returned to the living room, Dad pulled her close to slow-jam. I grabbed Lindsay and spun her around.

> *Girl, we're makin' it all come true.*
> *The time has come for me and you*
> *To rise on up to a brighter day....*
> *Oh girl, it's comin' true....*
> *Comin' true...comin' true...*

"Comin' True." The only old song I knew from the beginning to the end. Dad hummed that song lots of times. He had taught us all the words.

"Bennett, what's the *matter* with you?" Mom's beat followed Dad's lead.

"Don't talk, lady love. *Dance!* Can't a man be happy in his own house?"

> *A warm day's comin', shinin' new.*
> *Sunshine twinklin' for me and you.*
> *Oh girl, it's comin' true....*
> *Comin' true...comin' true...*

I broke into the Hump Back. Lindsay swung her bony hips to dance the Crunch. The music wrapped me so tight in its rhythm that I forgot why we were dancing. Then Dad turned down the volume. "Okay, you pretty ladies, sit down on the sofa. Your husband, and father"—Dad winked at me and Lindsay—"has some news. It's better than the lottery and the Redskins—combined."

The three of us squeezed onto our small sofa. Dad's feet shuffled to his own made-up footwork. "I got it," he said.

"You got it, what? The flu? Lovesickness?" I could tease as good as Dad.

Dad looked smug.

"You see, Dee, you're too smart for your own good," he said. "Just for that, I'm going to keep you guessing." Dad started snapping his fingers again. He went on with his dance.

"Why'd you have to start it with him, Dee? We'll be here guessing all *night*," Lindsay said.

"I didn't *have* to start. Dad made me do it. I get my smart-aleck behavior from him. Isn't that right, Mom? That's what you say all the time—'Just like your father.'"

Mom fingered a loose thread on the couch pillow. "Just like him," she agreed, giving my daddy a knowing look. Mom didn't need any more clues. "The job," she said.

Dad nodded and broke into a grin. "The job, baby."

Mom leapt off the couch to hug Dad. He straightened his glasses. "*Now* she wants to dance with me—now that I've been hired as vice president of special sales at the Kentwood Corporation, bottling division."

Mom smooched Dad's cheek. Her lipstick left puckery designs. Lindsay and I slapped a high five, though I didn't fully know why we were slapping. Excitement has a way of swirling me up and carrying me along for the ride, even before I know what the excitement is about.

I knew Dad had gone to New York City about a month before to interview for some big job. But when he came home from New York, all he said was, "Went well. Business is business." So I didn't give his trip another thought. Mom and Dad didn't say anything more about the job to me or Lindsay.

Tears moistened Mom's eyes. She said, "Bennett, I'm proud of you. You've worked hard for this."

"Grace, honey, this is our step—to finer, bigger, better. To comfort and safety."

I latched onto Mom and Dad's hug. Lindsay joined in too. "Kentwood's going to take good care of us," Dad said. "They'll arrange for the move, even help us find a new house."

I pulled away from our huddle. "What move?" I asked.

My feet stumbled backward. *"What move?"* I said it louder, then plunked onto the sofa. "What new house?" I raised my voice. "What *move,* what house? *Where?*"

Our fun, dancing, and hugs ended right there. Dad's announcement snagged Lindsay right after it hit me. She sat down, folded her arms, and swung one leg over the other. "We gonna be rich?" she wanted to know.

The laughter drained from Mom's face. But Dad's eyes still flickered with anticipation. Mom sat beside me and held my hand. "You didn't say anything about any *move* before," I said.

"No, we didn't. And we shouldn't talk about the details of this now." Mom's eyes pleaded with Dad. "Your father and I have to sort this out between us," she said.

A full week passed before Dad and Mom gave us the full story.

Dad pulled his TV-watching chair close to the sofa, where he asked me and Lindsay to sit. He said he had something "all-out wonderful" to tell us before bedtime. Mom settled on the arm of Dad's chair, holding what looked like a road map. Her expression wavered back and forth between pride and expectation.

"Girls, when both of you were babies, I made a vow to you and your mother." Dad's eyes had that same spark of promise they had had the week before. "I want you two to grow up knowing your daddy's given you a good start."

Mom handed the map to Dad. She looked down at her hands and turned her wedding ring around on her finger, over and over. "What your father's trying to say is—"

I slapped my hands over my eyes, as if I didn't want to see what I knew was coming. "We're moving," I said.

Dad pulled open the map and spread it over his lap, across the arms of his chair. "*Look*. Look at this. Wexford, Connecticut." Dad pointed to a small black dot on the map. "The landscaping is beautiful. You kids will have trees and a yard. There's even a place to ice-skate."

Goose pimples spread down my arms. All this talk about moving still stung like a fresh-ripped Band-Aid. I examined a patch of ashy skin on my elbow, trying to ignore the road map.

"I thought you said Kentwood is in New York City. How come we're moving *there*?" Lindsay's pointer finger landed on the crinkly map.

"We need a home tucked away from the noise and headaches of the city. After working in New York City all day, I want to come home to a place where the only sounds I hear at night are crickets," Dad said. "Besides," he continued, "I want to live in a town where I don't have to worry about you girls getting picked on. Remember when those foulmouthed kids roughed up that girl who lives over on Union Street?" Dad frowned. "Grace, what was that child's name—the one they beat up in the school yard?"

"Parker," Mom said, "I think her name was Robin Parker.

That little girl's mother hasn't been right ever since they put a bruising on her child."

"It's *Rhonda* Parker," I corrected. "And you're making a whole big thing out of nothing."

"That child is forever getting into fights," Mom said.

Lindsay said, "Oooh, I remember her last fight. It grew into an out-and-out war between her friends and some bigger girls who hang out near the playground at Rosa Parks Public."

"But that fight had nothing to do with me or Lindsay. The girls Rhonda beat up on, they should be the ones moving, not us," I argued.

"Our block isn't safe anymore. You girls shouldn't have it like this. My children need peace and quiet. And I need peace of mind," Dad said.

"How far away is Connecticut?" I forced myself to look at the map.

"Not more than a four-hour car ride," Mom answered.

"So are we gonna be rich or not?" Lindsay asked.

Dad made a playful tug on Lindsay's pigtail. "Just better off," he said.

Connecticut. A little black dot on a map, four hours away. The time it took to watch a double feature.

Lorelle's house stood on the corner of Redmond Avenue and Carver Place, less than a two-minute walk away. If it took four hours to drive to Connecticut—Mom said I couldn't get a driver's license until I turned eighteen—it probably took twenty-*times*-twenty hours to walk there.

Mom and Dad spewed out a whole bunch of praises about Connecticut. But no matter how hard they tried, their pie-in-the-sky promises didn't impress or convince me. And I told them so.

"Connecticut's got better schools," Dad said.

"I like the school I go to now!"

"This is a chance to live in the country," Mom said.

"The city suits me fine!"

Dad came back with, "It's safe. People don't lock their doors at night."

"Only stupid people leave their doors unlocked!" I snapped.

Mom said, "We can plant geraniums."

"I never even heard of geraniums!" was my answer to her.

Now, in our new house, I opened my eyes, not wanting to re-play any more of the scene. Mom and Dad had spelled it out pretty clearly on that night. We were moving, whether I'd heard of geraniums or not. And here we all were in Wexford, Connecticut.

Dad stirred on the sofa. His breathing grew faint and wheezy. Some dog barked outside and startled Dad awake. He tried to blink away sleep and bloodshot eyes.

"Dad, you know that song you're always singing, 'Comin' True'?" I asked.

The corners of Dad's mouth curled upward into a little smile. With his eyes closed to slits, he rocked his head side to side. Through a tired, crackly voice, he tried to sing, "Girl, we're makin' it all come true.... Rise on up to a brighter day...." The tune trailed off into Dad's half sleep. "I guess I'm losing my touch," he said softly.

4

Later that night, I perched on the edge of my bed. Each time I shifted my weight to balance myself, the coils in my box spring squeaked. The rickety noise was part of my room's rhythm, along with the steady ticking of my alarm clock.

I pounded my pillow, then propped it up against the head-board to make myself a back cushion. All the rooms in our house sat quiet. Outside, rain splotches plopped onto my window. Mom and Dad had turned in right after Dad had eaten his dinner. Dad had said he wanted to get a good night's sleep before facing another day of "the grind."

Lindsay and I were allowed to stay up until nine-thirty, when Mom and Dad trusted us to turn off our lights and go to sleep.

I folded my legs so that my nightgown draped into a little cradle, supported by my knees. There, I rested my camera, its lens staring up at me. I peered down, stuck out my tongue, and took a picture of my own face. That's when snatches of Mom and Dad's argument slithered under my bedroom door.

"C'mon, Grace. Let's not fight about this," Dad was saying.

"We're not fighting, Bennett, we're having a *discussion*." Their muted voices floated into my room. They tried to whisper, but I could still hear snippets of angry talk.

"…getting all worked up about nothing. That guy was on an ego trip…wasn't going to hurt me." Dad was starting to raise his voice.

"Bennett, *you* were on an ego trip. You shouldn't work late like you do."

I screwed the lens cap back on my camera and put the camera on the night table, next to my bed. My fingers fumbled beneath the shade of my bedside lamp, searching for the off switch. I snapped my bedroom into darkness and shoved myself between the cold sheets.

The only light that broke the pitch-black was the glow seeping from the hallway, under the crack of my bedroom door. Mom and Dad's heated words shot at me in the darkness. I huddled deeper under my covers.

"All right, Grace. *All right*," Dad said, lowering his voice. After that, I could hear only half sentences. "…in my office working late," Dad was saying. Then, "…as I was leaving…stopped me…going to the elevator…"

I heard Mom ask, "Then what?"

Dad said more muffled words, followed by "…told him I *worked* at Kentwood…that's what I told him, Grace."

I lay real still, straining to hear all I could. Mom's voice seemed to be growing more tense. I heard her say, "Bennett, you should have called someone right then." These bits of talk between Mom and Dad sent a shiver sliding through me.

I reached down under the covers and pulled up my socks.

My propped-up pillow landed on the side of my face. I yanked its softness in around my ears, but I could still make out some of the words between them.

"Who was I gonna call, Grace?" Dad was saying.

Silence.

Then I heard Dad say, "...backed me up in a corner...I slipped my hand in my breast pocket to get my wallet.... He got irrational...."

"Good God in heaven." Now Mom was speaking loudly.

Dad said, "Please, Grace, he was just working a power play." He was almost shouting.

Mom said, "Bennett, who knows what kind of evil that man had on his mind."

I could hear the sink running in the bathroom that connected with Mom and Dad's bedroom. I heard Mom splashing water, probably on her face. Dad called into the bathroom after her, loud enough for me to hear everything. "C'mon, Grace, it's the eighties, already. Doors are opening up for black folks like they never have before. This is what we marched for more than twenty years ago—a chance to walk through the door of opportunity."

The water stopped running, but it sounded as if Mom was still in the bathroom. She called back, "What about *our* doors, Bennett? What about *my* doors? What about the teaching job I left to walk with you down some unknown road?"

I beat my pillow into a mound and slammed my head on top. I rolled from my side to my back. Then I flipped onto my stomach, trying to settle into sleep. Nothing worked.

I tried to lie still and to keep listening. It sounded as if Mom was blowing her nose. "I miss home, Bennett," she said.

As the glow-in-the-dark hands on my clock inched toward

ten o'clock, my arms and legs took on the tired weight of iron pipes. I wanted to hug Mom and tell her I was sorry for acting moody that night in the kitchen.

I thought about Dad when he was a little boy, younger than me, delivering newspapers on a drizzly night like this one.

I loosened the hold on my pillow, letting my head settle into its cottony stuffing. With my body balled up in the dark, I could no longer see the rain outside. But as I drifted off to sleep, I heard it softly slapping the window.

On Saturday, two days after Mom and Dad's argument, I was out in the backyard watching Lindsay work her lacrosse stick.

Ch-click...I snapped my camera's shutter to get a good picture. "Why," I asked, "would anybody with any sense want to do *that*?"

"Look, Dee, to fit in here, you gotta play lacrosse. And you can't learn to play by taking pictures." Lindsay motioned me over. "Leave your camera on the steps, so I can show you how." I fit my camera into its case and jogged to where Lindsay stood on the grass. "Now, hold your stick like this and pull your elbows in closer to your body." She positioned my fingers around the stick.

Lindsay had learned lacrosse in a week by watching the other girls at her school prepare for tryouts. When she tried out for the Green Crest team, the coach chose her right away. Already, she was one of the school's top players. I asked her to teach me to play—to run up and down the grass, carrying a little ball in a net pouch connected to a stick—because lacrosse was the most popular sport at Wexford Middle School. The kids in Wexford liked lacrosse even more than basketball or kickball. I figured if I made the Wexford team, I'd fit in. Mom and Dad would think I liked Wexford. That would make them happy.

"Ow! That *hurt*!" The ball smacked against my thigh. I limped toward Lindsay. "Look, go easy on me. I got stuck with these Willis legs—the wrong kind for games like lacrosse," I said.

"C'mon. You never complained about your legs when you were high-stepping with the Jive Five. No one can touch you at rope, Dee. Not even me."

"That's because double-dutch is like dancing," I said.

"Well, then, *dance* down the lacrosse field. Because if the coach thinks you're nervous, you'll never make the team." Lindsay shifted her lacrosse stick back and forth in her hands. "Here, throw the ball to me and watch how I cradle it." She ran to the other side of the yard.

I tossed the ball toward Lindsay. It landed a long way from her feet and then rolled for another few inches.

"Dee, c'mon. You call that a throw? Be real." Lindsay scooped up the ball in the pouch of her lacrosse stick and jogged toward me.

"Here, hold your stick more like this," she said. "Turn it a little so the pouch faces outward." Lindsay showed me the right way. "And Dee, pay attention. Watch the ball at *all* times. I'll go back over there and throw the ball to you. Try to catch it with your stick."

"Wait—" I grabbed Lindsay's shoulder. "Wait a minute; there's something I want to ask you," I said. I looked straight at Lindsay. "How did you fit in so easy?"

Lindsay tossed the ball once in the air and caught it, almost without looking.

"Well, first I had to learn who was who. There's a girl,

Kippy Tate, who's the best lacrosse player on the team. I've seen her and her friends, other girls on the team, whispering stuff about me. Stuff I can't hear. But, see, I ignore them, because I know they're just talking junk."

I nodded, thinking about the girls on the school bus who were whispering about me. "The rest," Lindsay said, "is simple. I just pretend I'm white—I talk white. I walk white. It's that easy."

Talk white. Walk white. I had to think about that for a minute. I stared at Lindsay, praying she was making a joke. Sweat had pasted my glasses to the bridge of my nose. Lindsay wasn't sweating at all. When I realized that she was stone-cold serious, I said, "*White?* As coffee-colored as you are? Linds, you better leave that idea right here in this yard. The last thing you *are* is white. Pretending won't make those private school kids see you any differently."

"Look, Dee, I'm coffee with cream. And besides, all I'm doing is acting. *Acting,* so the Green Crest girls like me. What's the matter with that?"

"You're turning uppity, that's the matter with *that,*" I said. Lindsay shrugged. "Did you tell Mom and Dad you're trying to be white?" I asked.

"Get off it, Dee. I have something Green Crest needs—a lacrosse player with street smarts. Most of the girls at my school play pretty good. But they don't have the rhythm it takes to change up their pace on the field, to stay alive on their feet, like we used to do in double-dutch. The only other girl that scores more points than I do is Kippy Tate. Kippy 'Cradle' Tate, they call her."

"Just don't get too high on your pedestal, Linds. You know what pigeons do to statues," I said.

"What's the big deal? Maybe we should all act white. Then Mom wouldn't be so weepy, and she and Dad wouldn't argue like they been doing." Lindsay jammed her fist into the rawhide pouch of her lacrosse stick.

"Then you heard them the other night," I said.

Lindsay lowered her eyes. "I couldn't hear *every* word, but I *did* hear something about Dad's office and Mom missing back home," she said softly, digging the heal of her cleat into the grass.

"You hear anything else?" I asked.

"Nope. Just bits and pieces of talk is all." After a sigh, Lindsay added, "Mom and Dad always got along before."

For a moment me and Lindsay didn't say anything. I wondered if I should tell her what I'd heard about Dad being pushed into a corner. Then I remembered what we were doing in the yard in the first place. I said, "You think I got a chance at making the lacrosse team?" With my sweatshirt sleeve, I wiped the sweat off the bridge of my nose.

"Yeah. Just watch how they do it. Then, Dee, do it better."

"I don't know, Linds. This running back and forth isn't my thing."

"Don't worry, Dee. Those girls aren't gonna know what to do when Wexford Middle School's first black girl shows *them* how to play lacrosse. If you make the team, you're in. When I made the team at Green Crest, those stuck-up kids stopped staring at me like I had a beak."

"Serious?" I asked.

"Serious as a heart attack." Lindsay threw her lacrosse ball up again. She caught it with her knuckles bent firmly around the stick. "Now, go back over there and get ready for the ball," she said. "We got a lot of work to do!"

On the day of tryouts, I could hardly pay attention at school. I sat alone during lunch period. Mom and Dad's argument twisted and churned in my mind while I tried to remember what Lindsay had taught me about playing lacrosse—elbows in, eyes on the ball, dance down the field. I was eating a hot dog, minding my own business, when I heard his voice. That low moan sound, like the Swamp Water Man from the ghost stories Gebba used to tell.

"This seat taken?" Mr. McCurdy set down his lunch tray on my cafeteria table.

"Uh-uh. No, sir, I mean. It's not taken." I peeled my jacket off the back of the chair next to me.

"*Good*," he said in his weighty way of talking, "because these old bones are tired. I need to rest my limbs, and this looks like as good a place as any." I nodded and took a sip of my chocolate milk. My heart jumped faster than sneakers on pavement.

The grilled cheese sandwich on Mr. McCurdy's tray had stuck to its paper plate. Some of his coffee had stained his napkin. I moved my books and my camera off the small table to make more room. Mr. McCurdy lowered himself onto the wooden folding chair. He grumbled something about "blasted furniture," then said, "I had a camera once—a Brownie. Wasn't more than a brown metal box with a hole for looking. Not like those newfangled things they've got nowadays." He flung his fingers in the direction of my camera, which rested on a chair next to me. Mr. McCurdy's hands trembled, like Gebba's had. And the skin around his knuckles had little brown blotches. Liver spots, Gebba used to call them.

I picked at my hot dog and tried not to stare. "My dad gave me my camera for my birthday—last year, when I turned twelve," I explained.

"It suits you," he said, before taking a slow sip of coffee. I kept messing with my hot dog, not really eating, just nibbling at it. Some of the other kids in the cafeteria were watching our table—watching and pointing, and snickering. They're probably wondering why old-mule Mr. McCurdy and his grilled cheese sandwich are sitting here with me, I thought. Look at those kids, got nothing better to do.

Mr. McCurdy must have seen them carrying on. "I usually eat in the faculty lounge with the other teachers," he explained, "but the talk's all curriculum. Every now and then, a man needs a change of scene. Variety."

"Variety." I nodded agreement, too scared of those skin blotches and gnarly teeth to say otherwise. I didn't look at Mr. McCurdy's face—not once. I fiddled with my straw, played with the bottom of my sweater, folded my paper napkin. Anything to pass the time.

In his iron-barrel voice, Mr. McCurdy said, "I knew Langston Hughes."

My eyes shot up to meet his eyes—they were gray, like curb

cement—and I was looking straight at him. "*You* did?" I said. "For real?"

"I'm too old to lie—old as the bricks that built this school, I've been told—and I don't have time to waste making up stories."

"How'd *you* know Langston Hughes?" I asked.

"Knew him well, that's how."

"Yeah, but *how*? How'd you meet him—and where?"

Mr. McCurdy sipped more coffee. "My goodness, Miss Willis, you're awful curious all of a sudden. I guess the cat gave you back your tongue."

I took a bite of my hot dog and was careful not to talk too fast with food in my mouth. "I never met anybody who knows—knew, I mean—somebody famous."

Mr. McCurdy gave a little chuckle. "Hughes wasn't famous back in that day. Now don't get me wrong, some folks knew his name. But he was struggling like the rest of us college students, finding his voice and trying to get through school."

My hot dog had grown cold. I covered it with my napkin and slid my tray off to one side. I kept my chocolate milk nearby. "What college did you know Langston Hughes at?"

."James Mercer Langston Hughes—studied with him at Lincoln University, in Pennsylvania. We both finished up there in 1929. Hughes was smart as a whip. He could write the pants off all of us." Mr. McCurdy gulped more coffee.

I was silent, thinking about Langston Hughes—*James Mercer* Langston Hughes. After a moment, I said, "What else?"

"Hughes was always watching, *observing*, making notes in his mind, the way I see you doing." Mr. McCurdy was right about that. Since I'd come to Wexford, I'd collected a notebook full of stuff, all in my mind. Observations I couldn't wait to share with Lorelle.

Mr. McCurdy swallowed the last of his coffee. He hadn't touched his grilled cheese. From his pants pocket, he slid out a watch on a chain. "One-thirty," he said. "I need to be going."

But I didn't want Mr. McCurdy to go. I wanted to know more about Langston Hughes—and more about Mr. McCurdy. I stood up from my seat at the same time Mr. McCurdy rose from his chair. When he picked up his tray, I said, "You leaving?"

Mr. McCurdy brushed his wispy hair back over his balding head. His forehead had those liver spots too. "I'd better get on over to the faculty lounge—curriculum."

Those nosy kids watched Mr. McCurdy as he slid his cold grilled cheese sandwich and empty coffee cup into the trash bin near the EXIT sign and dragged his slow feet out the door. Then they turned to me and watched me drink the rest of my chocolate milk.

Just as I was about to dump my own lunch tray, I found another note, stuck to the underside of my knapsack. The handwriting was the same as before:

> *Mr. McCurdy's gross! Stay away!*
> *—Web*

I could smell the grass as we crossed the railroad tracks. Manley Tracks—the iron rails that carried Dad on a train between Connecticut and New York City—stretched out behind the Wexford Middle School gym. Just beyond the tracks, the land sloped down, then leveled off to make Manley Field.

About fifty girls showed up for lacrosse tryouts. We jogged toward the field in an uneven V, like geese in flight. The better players—girls with worn lacrosse sticks—headed the group. I kept up at the rear. Out of the corner of my eye, I could see that red-haired girl from English class. Her lacrosse stick looked as new as mine.

A hay fever sneeze shook my whole head. I snatched a wad of Kleenex tucked into the sweatband around my wrist. As I squished through the muddy grass, my new cleats pinched at my toes and heels, worse than new Easter shoes. When we reached the field, I knelt down to loosen the laces, careful not to let my knees smack into the mud. I gripped my lacrosse stick in one hand and balanced my camera under my arm. I wasn't going to leave my camera in the locker room. And I sure wasn't going to leave it on the bench. I'll have to do lacrosse with it—some kind of way, I thought.

"Okay, ladies, count off by tens!" When the lacrosse coach blew on her gym whistle, her neck disappeared into her double chin. Everybody called her Renner, not *Coach* Renner or *Miss* Renner. Just *Renner.* "Once you've counted, break into groups according to your number. We'll start off with drills!" Renner shouted. Needle pricks from nervous sweat stung my armpits. I sneezed again.

"I want all the even-numbered girls at the other end of the field. Odds, over there!" I could hear Renner from behind. Then a heavy hand tapped my shoulder. "You're not going to need that camera here." Renner was holding out her fleshy palm. I looked up into her thick face and handed her my camera. "You're an odd," Renner said. "Over there!" She pointed.

My hay fever was acting up bad. My nose threw out a bunch of sneezes, one right after the other. The tissue in my wristband was no good. It had mopped up all the sweat on my wrist. So I sniffled back a glob of snot and wiped up the rest with the back of my hand. I swallowed hard while I jogged to my place on the grass.

"Okay, ladies, *move it*! Drop your sticks and circle twice, from one goalpost to the other." Renner's baseball cap said DO OR DIE across the front.

With the rest of the odds, I started a slow jog. Halfway around the field, I fought for breath. And my sore feet showed me no mercy.

"Deirdre Willis, right?" Renner was trotting alongside me, checking my name off on her clipboard. "Willis. Right," I said. Renner blew out quick breaths. "Keep breathing, Willis. This is just a warm-up." My camera hung around Renner's neck. While she jogged, it bounced off her bosom. "Don't worry, this baby is safe with me." She gave my camera case a pat, like for a newborn's bottom. I nodded. Renner ran ahead, screeching her whistle.

Already, the warm-up was stomping me down. I couldn't understand it. Double-dutch never made me tired. Back home when I taught the younger girls double-dutch, I jumped from right after school till dinnertime almost every day. My legs could take any quickstep Lorelle put out. When my feet weaved between the ropes, I never quit. Even when Mom called me in to eat, I had enough left in me to go at least ten more jumps. We jumped the Salt Shaker, the Triple Time Line, and Hell Heel. Lorelle could jump Hell Heel all the way through without tripping once.

Renner sounded her whistle again. "Warm-up's over!" Then she lined us up single file. "Listen up! When I throw the ball to the first girl in line, she catches it in her pouch, tosses it back to me, then runs to the end of the line. Any questions?"

I stood fifth in the single line, leaning sideways out of the line to get a look at the girls ahead of me. One girl caught the ball, then spun her stick twice before shooting the ball back to Renner.

When my turn came up, I tried to use the moves Lindsay taught me. But I couldn't remember if I was supposed to keep my elbows tight and my eyes on the ball or if I was supposed to keep my eyes on my elbows. I watched the ball to make sure it didn't knock me upside my head. But the ball flew at me so fast, I ducked. On my next turn, I swung my stick, afraid the ball would smash my glasses. Instead, it cracked against my stick's handle. All I could do was bunt it back.

I was sent to the bench, where I had to squeeze in between the six other girls who'd also been put off the field. Renner ran away with my camera before I could even catch my breath to ask her for it. Disappointment at not making it through the drill—and at not getting my camera back—swallowed me up whole. It was clear from the get-go, I thought. No way I'm gonna make the team now.

And to make matters worse, I'd ended up next to the red-haired girl from English. I fumbled with my shoelaces, pretending not to notice her. That dumb smirk never left her face, and she eyeballed me even more than she had on that first day in class. Finally, I couldn't stand her staring. "What are you *looking* at?" I asked. "And what's so funny?"

She dug the pole of her lacrosse stick into the dirt. "Last year when I tried out for this stupid team, I didn't even make it through that drill. The ball shot me in the shoulder and I screamed so loud, they sent me home. I still got a bruise—*see*." She yanked back her sleeve, but all I saw on her arm were freckles.

Her eagle eyes made me nervous, but I kept a straight face—no blinking, lips tight—so she wouldn't know it. I stared straight ahead at a scrimmage game on the field, watching for Renner and my camera.

Even with the noise of Renner's whistle, I could hear what's-her-name, the redhead, chomping. "Want some gum?" she asked. "It's Banana Bubble, my last piece." She poked a shiny foil package under my nose.

"No thanks." I snuck glances at her mouth to get a better look at how she chewed. Back at Rosa Parks Public, we had a name for chewing like that. We called it doing the jawbone. And, I thought, she's doing the double-time jawbone.

This girl worked on her Banana Bubble so fast, it flew out of her mouth and smacked into the dirt. She picked up the yellow glob and examined it carefully. Without a second thought, she blew on the gum and popped it back in her mouth.

"That's nasty," I said.

"It may be nasty to you, but good gum is hard to find—not worth wasting, you know what I mean? Besides, I saw you wipe your nose with the back of your hand, and that's *nastier* than nasty."

She had a point. But I wasn't giving it to her. "I couldn't help it," I said. "I ran out of tissue."

"Well, I ran out of gum. So we're even."

Lorelle had warned me about white girls with an attitude. And this white girl, with her jawbone, was one of them. Doesn't know nothing about Langston Hughes, either, I thought. I shrugged and got up to find another place on the bench. I couldn't be bothered with a smarty-pants.

"Hey, where you going? This bench is full. And you know what they say—you move, you lose."

The only place I'd heard that line before was on the Redmond Avenue bus when someone was stupid enough to give up a perfectly good seat.

"Looks like you and me *already* lost." She gestured toward the field with her chin. "Renner kicked us out of the game before we even got started," she said.

That show-off player from our drill line was spinning her stick as she ran down the field, about to score. I sucked my teeth. She's probably got an attitude too.

"That's Stacy Snead. Her brother's this big jock head up at Yale. He taught her everything about lacrosse. I don't know why she even bothers coming to tryouts."

Attitude or not, that Stacy girl could *move*.

I recognized some of the girls from my school bus—eyes shifting, taking me in, making up their minds about me spending time with Miss Jawbone. *Attitudes with a capital* A. That's what Lorelle would've said about them.

The redhead kept on. "Last year, after that lacrosse ball slugged me, Renner said, 'Web, some of us are cut out for lacrosse and some of us aren't.'"

I had split my attention among Stacy whipping her stick, Renner running up and down with my camera, and this Banana Bubble girl throwing out small talk.

It took me a minute, but then I got it. *Web.* I should have known.

"*You're* Web," I said. "You put that note on my chair in English class and the one on my knapsack today in the cafeteria without me seeing. You left me out in the cold—left me hanging, wondering who you were." I rested my hand on my hip.

Web blew a bubble with her dirty gum. "Well, now you know—*I'm* Web."

"I'm D—" I started to say my name.

"You're *brave* is what *you* are," Web said. "Standing up in front of our class on your first day, talking the way you did about Langston Hughes—and impressing Mr. McCurdy. And then eating lunch with him. You got *guts*."

I shrugged. "What's up with Mr. McCurdy? How come you called him gross?"

"'Cause he *is* gross. He's ancient—and wrinkly and has old-people spots, and he's *scary*."

"He only looks and sounds scary. But he's regular," I said.

"A regular spook face," Web said.

I tried to explain that Mr. McCurdy was cool, but I couldn't speak any more than a few words before Web started running off at the mouth again. "This gum thing's a bad habit, hard to kick. I've tried to cut down, chew sugarless. But I'm up to two packs a day." Web's teeth grew in as even as piano keys. And for somebody who chewed so much gum, those teeth were white as rice. Her tongue slid out the side of her mouth when she spoke and chewed at the same time. "You ever get heavy into gum?" she asked.

I shook my head. "No."

Lorelle once told me the best way to slow up a girl with a busy mouth (and an attitude) is to throw her onto another subject. "Where you get a name like Web?" I folded my arms.

"Web's after my grandma, Hilda Weber. See, my parents gave me her last name as a first name. My full name's Weber Coile—Web, I like to be called."

I took my arms down off my chest. "I got a grandma name too. Deirdre Willis," I said. "Deirdre was *my* grand's name. We called her Gebba Willis, though. People call me Dee. Dee Willis. Or Camera Dee, 'cause I take a lot of pictures."

Just like that, Web stopped talking. After a moment, she said, "My grandma's passed away."

"So's mine," I said.

I looked down toward the other end of the field. Renner was way over by the grassy hill that led to the train tracks. She still had my camera, and I was itchy to get it back. But she was too far away for me to holler. Besides, I was afraid *she'd* holler at *me* if I got up off the bench.

"That Renner lady's something else," I said.

"*Lacrosse* is something else."

"Why do you bother trying out at all?"

"Because. There are two traditions in Wexford—lacrosse and 'sembly. In this town, both are as important as Thanksgiving. 'Sembly's fun, so I know why it's a big deal. But lacrosse, that's another story. I try out for lacrosse because I'm still trying to figure out what the big deal is."

"And 'sembly, what's that?" I asked, saying a silent prayer: Please don't let it have to do with grass and running up and down.

"'Sembly is short for the Founders' Day *Assembly,* our Wexford Middle School annual talent contest. Kids just call it 'sembly." Web was back to working her jawbone, talking and chewing without a rest. "It's like this," she said. "On the first Friday night in June, all the kids bring their talents to perform in the school auditorium. Some sing songs. Others do ballet from the lessons they've taken at the Wexford Graces School. Kids bring instruments, costumes, all kinds of stuff."

I didn't give a toe bone about some Founders' Day Assembly, but Web tried to convince me to enter. I shook my head. "I can only sing good with the radio. I don't play any instruments. As far as dancing goes, I save my rhythm moves for parties. And Web, being in a contest with the kids at this school would be *no* party," I said.

Still, Web talked up 'sembly this and 'sembly that. I let her go on and on, because while she spoke, I watched. I used it as *my* turn to check *her* out.

Web's lips drew a thin pink line across her face, except for when she wrinkled them into one of her smirks. Bangs stopped just below her eyebrows and her hair hung as straight as string. The uppity black kids in Baltimore used to say that white hair was "good" hair, manageable and easy to comb. Black hair, they said, was "bad" hair—kinky and nappy, they called it. As tight-curled as it is, I've always liked my hair. Besides, Jell-O is *good;* fighting on the playground is *bad*. Hair is just hair.

Web's breasts poked through her T-shirt, and I could see the outline of a lacy bra. At home I had a drawer full of training bras that Lindsay was always stealing—and stuffing.

For a few minutes, I'd forgotten Renner still had my camera, until she ran toward me, letting my camera dangle on its strap. That's when I lost interest in Web's looks and her 'sembly story. Renner ran up to me at the bench. "Here's your sharpshooter," she said, handing me my camera. Then she said, "Deirdre, some of us are cut out for lacrosse and some of us aren't." And she ran back to the field, blowing her whistle.

"Don't mind her, Dee," Web said. "She's a fanatic. She wears that 'Do or Die' cap like it's a mink coat." I was too busy checking my camera case for scratches to care about Renner or to listen to any more from Web. I unsnapped the camera case and carefully unscrewed my lens cap. As I looked toward the end of the field, my lens pulled Stacy Snead into focus. That's when I *saw* lacrosse.

The spin on Stacy's lacrosse stick showed off her handwork. *Ch-click*...I snapped Stacy's picture. Whipping across the field from one stick's pouch to another, the lacrosse ball carried a white blur behind it. *Ch-click*...I captured the stream of action with one shutter snap. The players, toughing it out on the slippery field as a train dashed by on the horizon, made the kind of

stop-action photo that I saw only in magazines. *Ch-click...
ch-click.*

"Hey, let *me* see!" Web gave me a nudge. Not wanting to
miss a single shot, I leaned closer to Web—my camera strap still
around my neck—and braced my shoulder against hers. Gently,
I helped Web curl her fingers around the lens. "Hold the lens
like this, then turn it *slowly.*"

Stacy Snead spun her stick faster (Web told me that was
called cradling). With the ball in her stick's pouch and her teeth
clenched, she sprinted down the field. "Shoot it!" I yelled at
Web. *"Shoot!"*

"You mean push the button, take the picture?" Web
squinted one eye and played with the focus. The squishy field
was no match for the speed on Stacy's cleats.

"Yeah, I mean *push* the button! *Take the picture!*" I
shouted. Just before Stacy dived toward the goalie, Web caught
the shot. Carefully, she handed back my camera, then blew a
bubble. I slapped her a high five. We'd finished off the roll of
film.

"You shoot pretty good," I said, fitting a new spool of film
into my camera.

"You teach how to shoot pretty good, and I bet your pictures come out great." Web's expression turned intent, as if she
was getting an idea. "You should enter 'sembly with your photos, Dee. You can make an exhibit, hang all your pictures up in
a display," she suggested.

I slid my eyes sideways toward Web. That's when she explained, "Last year, Stacy Snead won the Founders' Day Assembly for demonstrating what she called 'The Snead Cradle.'
She did a whole ball-and-stick routine, right in the auditorium."

I sucked my teeth. "*That's* a talent-show talent?"

"To her—and to last's years's judge—it was."

I shrugged. "No 'sembly for me."

"Okay, okay, I won't push it for now," Web said, "but one thing's for sure. With your camera, we showed 'Do or Die' that we can *do* lacrosse without dropping dead." Web cracked her gum in the back of her teeth.

"Doesn't she think we *know* we're not cut out for lacrosse?" she said. "I don't let her get away with all her pep-talk business. You got to watch it here, Dee. All this Wexford status stuff can make you crazy, if you let it. These snobs drove my cat into a deep depression. She was fine before we moved here. Now she's a mental case."

I threw one of Web's lopsided looks back at her.

"No, seriously," she said. "When we moved here from Queens three years ago, my cat, Fluffy, thought she was still in New York City. First our big front yard freaked her out, then she got lost on our never-ending driveway. And all those *trees.* Fluffy couldn't take it. Fire escapes were more her style."

"Me and Fluffy got a lot in common," I said. A giggle escaped from my throat, then another from deeper down. I cupped my hand over my mouth.

Web laughed too. "Then Fluffy saw this other cat from next door in our yard. The other cat was wearing one of those designer plaid cat coats—probably a family heirloom passed on through the generations. Fluffy couldn't take it. She came meowing home, and now she won't leave the house. Poor thing. I think it's because my parents refuse to buy her a cat coat. Designer coats cost money, you know."

A designer cat coat. I laughed so hard, I had to gasp for breath, and I snorted every time I tried to speak.

Web nudged me with her shoulder. "Hey, take my picture," she said. "Imagine me with the cat coat—plaid."

I drew deep breaths to calm myself down, afraid I'd explode with more laughter if I tried to talk too fast. "Only"—giggle—"if you stop yakking. As much as you talk, there's gonna be a blur on your lips in the picture."

"Okay, okay, okay, okay. Here, my mouth is shut, lips still. No more talking."

I took two shots—*ch-click...ch-click*—one for me, one to send to Lorelle.

"Hey, Dee," Web said, "try not to take it too hard when Renner breaks us the news—we're not gonna make the lacrosse team." Web looked out at the girls left playing on the field. "Fluffy will be so disappointed." She sighed.

"So will Lindsay, my sister," I said.

"Does she like cats?"

"No, but she loves lacrosse and designer clothes. And Wexford's sending her way off the deep end, like Fluffy."

For the rest of the afternoon, Web and I relaxed into the first warm day of spring. The icy lump that had been nestling in my throat since we'd come to Wexford melted. My hay fever sneezes dried up. And I did more giggling with a girl named Web.

6

I came through the back door, into the kitchen. "Dee, honey, is that you?" Mom called to me from upstairs.

"It's the hungry burglar!" I called back as I checked out our refrigerator shelves. Mom hollered, "I'm up here, unpacking the last of the boxes. Eat a piece of fruit or something, but don't spoil your appetite for dinner."

It was too late. I'd already found the Jell-O and was spooning whipped cream on top. Mom had made a batch with tiny fruit-cocktail cubes. I tried to pick out a few extra chunks with my spoon—pieces of fruit that wouldn't spoil my appetite.

Before I sat down to enjoy my Jell-O, I tied my cleats by their laces onto the head of my lacrosse stick. I propped the string-and-leather contraption in the corner. Upstairs, Mom's footsteps creaked the floorboards. "Oh, and Dee, honey," Mom called, "there's a surprise for you on the kitchen table."

As I sucked a peach morsel off my spoon, the surprise snagged my eye. FOR DEE'S EYES ONLY. That's what was written on the front of an envelope, which bulged at its edges. I didn't need to look at the return address printed in the left-hand corner to know the letter had come from Lorelle.

With my spoon pressed between my tongue and the roof of my mouth, I ripped open the envelope's top seam. Inside were two pages of notebook paper wrapped around some bent-up snapshots. I unfolded the letter but left the photos alone. I knew that if I thumbed through the pictures first, I'd start crying, remembering good times gone forever.

Lorelle was one of the few people whose handwriting looked as neat as typewriter print. Her letter began:

So Dee, was I right?

White kids everywhere, I bet. Hanging out like the socks on Mrs. Parnell's clothesline. Kids with an attitude a mile high. Aren't you glad you picked public school over that Green Crest place your parents wanted you to go to with Lindsay? Are the white kids at a regular school less uppity than private school kids?

I was telling Rhonda Parker the other day (she and me are close now) how your parents wanted both you and Lindsay to go to Green Crest Academy. Rhonda cracked up when I explained to her how you laid it down for your mom and dad, told them you weren't moving to Connecticut unless they let you go to the school you wanted.

Are you glad you stood your ground, Dee? Are you glad you listened to me? Because I know about these things. I'm your girl and would never steer you wrong. It's like I told you, my cousin went to one of those academies and the white kids treated her like she was gutter dirt. She said those prep schools disrespect black people. Knowing Lindsay, though, she won't let them—or nobody—do her wrong.

I've been pretty good, but the Jumpin' Jive Five isn't the same since you left. When you moved, we only had four Jive Fivers. But on account of her fast feet, we let Rhonda join our team. Rhonda's smooth, Dee. That girl can really jump good! And she helps me think of new routines for the younger girls. But Dee, Rhonda can get evil sometimes. I'm her friend now, and I'm trying to teach her not to fight so much. Sometimes she listens to me. Sometimes she acts up, anyway.

A shudder zigzagged inside my belly. I yanked my spoon out of my mouth. "Lorelle, you let *Rhonda* take *my* place on the Jive Five?" The question shot out from under my breath, and I couldn't help but whisper a curse. I followed the sentences of Lorelle's letter with my finger to make sure I was reading right.

Last week me and Rhonda made up this double-dutch jump we call Groove Move. It's even harder than Hell Heel, if you can believe that. We're planning to enter this year's Street Fest contest. They say it's going to be the biggest block party competition Redmond Avenue has ever seen. If we win, we get to go to Washington, D.C., to compete with kids from all over the country.

How do you like Connecticut so far? Have you met any kids yet? What kind of double-dutch do they do there? Please write and tell me all about it.

I turned my eyes toward my lacrosse stick in the corner. Then I pressed the creases out of Lorelle's letter and kept reading.

Dee, I put some pictures in the envelope. They're the ones you took of the Jumpin' Jive Five last summer at the block party. Check out the one with me doing Hell Heel. The way that picture shows off my legs makes me look *good*. The only problem is, my hair wouldn't lay down that day. Mama said I could get my hair braided, like you and me said we were gonna do. But I'm thinking I want a perm instead, so my edges will lay smooth.

Dee, what do you think I should do with my hair? Also, I want to know all about Connecticut.

Oh, Dee. One last thing. You want to come and visit this summer? Mama and Aunt Vonette said you can stay with us. Me and Rhonda can teach you Groove Move.

Say hi to Lindsay and your mom and dad for me.

> Your J-Five girl, and friend to the end,
> Lorelle

P.S. I got my period! It made me get some cramps.

I folded Lorelle's letter and tucked it back in its envelope without looking at the pictures.

With quick little chops, I mashed my Jell-O with the tip of my spoon, waiting for tears to choke my throat and pool up in my eyes. But my tears stayed hidden. They took their own time. I missed Lorelle more than anything, but in the month since I'd moved away, things had already changed—things that made Lorelle seem like a person from another world.

First of all, Lorelle was going for a perm, which we said we'd *never* do. And how could Lorelle even *think* of hanging with Rhonda Parker? Rhonda was trouble. Lorelle had changed that way, too. She and Rhonda. *Friends.*

I slid Lorelle's letter from its envelope and read over the part about going to Washington, D.C., to the double-dutch competition. I knew the Jumpin' Jive Five could win that contest with the jumps *I* taught them. But if Rhonda Parker joined the Jive Fivers, she'd mess up everything. She'd probably get up in the judge's face and start a fight. Lorelle and the J-Jive Five would get kicked out of the competition for sure.

Soft, like a daydream, I heard the J-Jive Five rhyme sneaking up on my thoughts. It sang to me like an echo far, far away.

> *We call ourselves the Jumpin' Jive Five.*
> *When we get down, the rope comes alive.*
> *Jumpin' over the moon. Jumpin' over the sun.*
> *Got two ropes twirlin' instead of one!*

That's when my tears came. Slow at first. Then steady.

Outside the kitchen window, shrubs were beginning to bloom. In the thick of our backyard's leafiest bush, a robin fed worms to just-hatched babies. I stared out the window at the pale sky, noticing that the days were staying light longer.

Back home, Lorelle was probably on the corner of Redmond and Carver, jumping fast rhythms until her mama called her in from the street.

With my fingers, I smeared away my tears. I fished for another peach cube buried somewhere in my warm Jell-O, then went to the refrigerator to pile cold Jell-O into my bowl. Mom's favorite HOME SWEET HOME magnet clung to the freezer door. It had lost some of its grip and hung like a lopsided medallion. The magnet held a scrap of paper, a note from Mom that said:

Dee, before you came home, someone named Web called. She said she wanted to talk to you about the sembly (she said you'd know what that means). Her number is 555-1483.

—Mom

A few minutes later, Lindsay pounded up the back porch steps. She stomped into the kitchen, peeled off her Green Crest JV jacket, and stormed toward the steps that led from the kitchen to her bedroom. She didn't even notice me sitting at the kitchen table.

Halfway up the stairs, Lindsay bumped into Mom, who was coming downstairs with an armful of laundry. "Hold it there, child. Where do you think you're going in such a hurry? You're a sight!" Lindsay struggled past Mom without looking up. "What on earth happened to your hair?" Mom set her laundry load down on a stair step and held Lindsay out in front of her to get a better look. Lindsay's pigtails had come unraveled. Her hair stuck out in a crinkly mess, as if she'd been caught in a rainstorm or had just stepped out of the shower. And her hair ribbons were gone.

Lindsay tried to smooth the tangled strands with her fingers. "I got dirt in my hair during lacrosse practice. I had to rinse it out. Now let me go upstairs," she said, ducking under Mom's arm.

"Not so fast," Mom said. "If there was dirt in your hair, then Lord knows, those lacrosse clothes must be soiled something awful. Throw that gym bag right on top of this pile, before I head for the washer." Lindsay hugged her gym bag under one arm. Mom wrestled it away from her, and set it on top of the load resting on the stair.

I tried to lighten Lindsay's dark mood. "C'mon, Linds, sit down next to me." I held up a spoonful of Jell-O. "Here, I'll feed you some of this while I tell you about my lacrosse tryouts. Those tryouts were *funny*, Linds. I met this girl who told me the craziest story about her cat, *Fluffy*—" Web's cat-coat story still cracked me up. I couldn't finish it without giggling. But Lindsay didn't want to hear it. She pressed her lips tightly together and gave me a sharp look. Her eyes were rimmed in red. I tried again to make her smile. "Look at my stick-and-cleat statue over there," I said. "It's wearing string-and-leather fashion."

Lindsay cut an evil eye to the corner where my cleats and stick stood. Then, in a shot, she slipped around Mom's waist and ran up the rest of the stairs. Before she disappeared into her room, she called out, "That might be funny to *you*. But do I look like I'm *laughing*?"

Mom's eyes searched my face for some kind of answer. I shrugged. "Don't ask me," I said.

Mom unzipped Lindsay's gym bag and turned it upside down. Out tumbled Lindsay's lacrosse shorts, T-shirt, and socks. They were clean and folded, as if she hadn't worn them at all.

7

Lindsay swore she had outgrown her stuffed bear, Ted. But that night when I poked my face into Lindsay's half-open bedroom door, she was holding Ted tight.

I knocked softly, pushing the door at the same time. "Linds, it's me, Dee. Can I come in?"

Lindsay sat on her bed, legs folded. By holding Ted's raggedy arms, she flipped him over in slow somersaults. "You're already in," she said. I stood at the foot of Lindsay's bed and curled my fingers around her bedpost. "It's your turn to sweep up the kitchen. Mom told me to hunt you down."

Lindsay tucked Ted in her lap, the same way she used to when she was little, in the days when she called Ted Cuddle Bear. "I don't feel like sweeping," she said. "Tell Mom I'm sick."

"You just ate two lamb chops and a plateful of mashed potatoes—and limas. How sick is sick?" I eased onto the corner of the bed.

"Sick enough to be left alone." Lindsay sprawled onto her

side. She started picking lint from Ted's matted ear fur, ignoring me.

Bacon, the stuffed piglet I'd passed down to Lindsay, lay at the foot of the bed. I reached over and uncurled Bacon's tail. Lindsay and I used to love playing with Bacon and Ted. When we were little, we pulled Bacon's tail out straight, then got lost in our own laughter as we watched the tail spring back to a curlicue.

Gently, I wiggled Bacon under Lindsay's nose. I tried to talk pig talk, like we used to do. "What you sick about, Lindsay Lou?"

Lindsay concentrated on Ted's fur. She picked more lint and smoothed the felt patches on Ted's paws. She didn't look up, just said, "Stop it, Dee. Get that pig out of my face."

When we were little, Bacon could always make Lindsay laugh. "But Lindsay Lou"—I pressed Bacon's snout to Lindsay's nose—"it's me, *Bacon*." Lindsay sucked her teeth. I rested Bacon beside Ted, near Lindsay. Softly, I asked, "What's wrong, Linds?"

Lindsay looked straight at me, her expression so serious, it made me blink. "Today when I came home from school with my hair messed up?" I nodded. "*Today* made me sick, Dee." With Ted in her lap, Lindsay sat up and swung her feet around so they dangled off the side of the bed. I scooted closer.

"Some of the kids at Green Crest have made me sick. Most of them treat me okay. And the teachers don't bother me, because I do my schoolwork. But Dee, some of those lacrosse team girls are *mean*." Lindsay's forehead wrinkled into a frown. I took a deep breath.

"Remember I told you how some of the girls had started whispering stuff about me? How one of them, Kippy Tate, is one of the best players and all?" I nodded, thinking back to the day Linds tried to teach me to play lacrosse in the yard, when she told me she was figuring out who was who at school. "Well, I've been scoring better than Kippy. And after a while," Lindsay said, "it seemed like Kippy and her friends were scheming, planning something.

"Like I told you," she went on, "I tried to ignore it at first, not let them get to me. They're all just jealous of me anyhow, because I can run *and* cradle *and* score, as easy as I can brush my teeth."

"You *can*," I agreed, leaning the back of my head onto the bedpost.

"But Dee, today—when I came home with my hair flying out in all directions—some of those girls had challenged me in the locker room before practice. They dared me, made a bet. Kippy said, 'You think you're hot snot, don't you? Well, let's see you wash that Brillo frizz out of your hair.'"

My eyes grew wide as Lindsay let go with her story. "What then?" I asked.

"Kippy's the one who made the dare, Dee. She said I could change my hair if I rinsed it under hot sink water. I told her and her friends, Heather Fink and Dolores Brewster, that water couldn't wash out the way my hair is. I told them nothing could—it's a texture thing."

Right then, I thought back to Lindsay saying she was gonna act white. I took another deep breath, because I knew from the day she'd said it that it was a bad idea. Now acting white had caught up with her.

"And you took on the dare?" I asked.

"I knew what they were saying was crazy, and I told them it'd never work, rinsing my hair to make it straight. But they kept coming at me, Dee. Messing with my thinking. Kippy said, *'Prove it.'*

"Our coach had already gone out to the field, and those girls knew it was just us in the locker room. Then Heather and Dolores followed Kippy, and the two of them kept saying it over and over. *'Prove it! Prove it! Prove it!'*" Lindsay stopped talking to catch her breath. When she spoke again, she dropped her voice almost to a whisper.

"So...," she stammered, "I unbraided my hair...and stuck my head under the hottest sink water I could stand...."

Lindsay exhaled slowly. "My hair looked ugly, Dee. And the only thing I *proved* was that from now on I'm gonna have to play triple good at lacrosse so that I can *prove* to everybody that they'd better not bother me, because I'll run all of them off the field if I have to!"

Lindsay squeezed her eyes shut. She buried her face in Ted's belly, and for the first time since we'd moved to Wexford, I saw my sister cry. "After it happened"—Lindsay kept her face pressed to Ted's fur—"I told the coach I had a stomachache. I packed my gym clothes in my bag and came home. That's when I ran into the kitchen, acting evil to you and Mom."

I curled my arm around Lindsay's shoulders, the way Mom always did to me when I cried. "Linds," I said softly, "it'll be okay." But my words were only pieces of a promise. I didn't really know if it *would* be okay.

Lindsay sucked in short breaths, the half breaths of weeping from deep down. "I'm a crybaby," she said.

I hugged Lindsay a little closer. "Go ahead, Linds. Cry all you want."

Now moving to Wexford had hurt all of us in some way, even Lindsay, who could stand up to just about anybody. Lindsay sniffled and wiped her face on the bedspread. "I know I should speak up, say something to put those girls in their place." From where we sat on the bed, I could see Lindsay's reflection in her dresser mirror, across the room. Her shoulders—broad ones like Mom's—slouched beneath her shirt. "But I'm afraid anything I say will screw up things for Mom and Dad," she explained. "They're paying a lot of money for Green Crest. And you know what they used to say back on the block...." We said it at the same time: "The only green that grows on trees is leaves."

"But Linds," I said, "letting kids pick on you is no good."

Lindsay reached over and pulled on Bacon's tail. As the tail coiled back, her expression loosened. I smoothed Ted's tummy fur. It was damp from Lindsay's tears. For a moment, neither of us spoke. Ted and Bacon lay still.

"You should tell Mom and Dad about Green Crest, Linds. About what happened with those girls," I said.

"*No.* They got enough stuff to deal with. And I'm not taking Dad's dream away. He wants me and you and Mom to be happy here."

"But maybe Mom and Dad can talk to your coach and tell her about some of the nasty kids at school," I suggested.

"No, Dee. *No.*" Lindsay wrapped her arms around Ted's pudgy brown body. "I'm one of the best girls playing lacrosse at Green Crest, and the one who's scored the most points so far this season.

"Dee, last week when we played Norton Country Day School, I scored *four* points. I might even get to play varsity lacrosse next year. *Varsity,* Dee—with upper-school girls. That would make Mom and Dad prouder than proud."

"Linds, they'll be more proud if you tell them—"

"Dee, if Mom and Dad go snooping around, complaining to the coach, the other girls at Green Crest will call me a troublemaker. They won't give me a chance.

"The way I see it," Lindsay went on, "I've got two choices. One is to shut up and put up. The other is to *speak* up, and *mess* things up for Mom and Dad—and me."

"But Linds—"

Lindsay stuck out her pinky to do the Redmond Avenue pinky handshake. "Promise me you won't tell Mom and Dad about Kippy Tate and her mean jokes. I'll work it out myself," she said. "I need you to look out for me, Dee. Promise, Dee. Please."

Lindsay's eyes were still puffy from crying. I hooked my pinky with hers. "Promise," I said.

8

In the morning, I left our house a half hour early so that I could take pictures of the sun winding its way up Scarlet Oak Lane.

As I walked along our barren street, looking for sights to shoot, I thought back to the mornings on Redmond Avenue, where folks from the neighborhood greeted each other with a friendly "How you do?" I used to meet Lorelle on her front stoop at eight. Lorelle's aunt Vonette would be waiting with buttery slices of sugar toast to start the day off right. Then me and Lorelle, we'd walk to Rosa Parks Public, meeting up with other kids along the way.

Scarlet Oak Lane was a whole different scene.

Our neighbors—people I'd never met—lived in houses set back off the road, houses secluded by trees. Homes kept at a deliberate distance from each other. "Suburban privacy" is what Dad called it.

At the end of Scarlet Oak, a low stone wall separated the street from the woods. I leaned against the wall and listened to the sound of no sound—no cars, no kids, no neighbors sending me a "How you do?" The damp air hung silent. To me, it was too much quiet for a morning at rush hour.

There was lots to see, though. Lots to make good pictures. I slid my camera from its case and rested the case on the stone wall. The sun's glare lighted the dew on the leaves, making the trees in the distance twinkle like a forest of crystal-drop chandeliers.

Ch-click...ch-click...ch-click.

Tiny spiderwebs decorated the wall's jagged stones. One of the webs cradled a sleeping spider. Another shimmered like silk lace in the light.

Ch-click...ch-click...ch-click.

Just beyond the clearing, I heard the leaves rustle. Somebody was approaching from the woods. I stepped away from the wall, afraid I was trespassing on someone else's property. That's when I spotted a doe coming toward me through the trees. Her coat was velvet-smooth, her eyes big and round and friendly.

We both stood real still, admiring each other from a safe distance. I carefully lifted my camera to my face. As I focused my lens, the doe's eyes turned cautious. "How you do?" I whispered. Then, "You're a beautiful brown lady. Can I please take your picture?" And as if she knew how truly special she was, she let me snap the shutter. When I advanced my film and went for another shot, she turned back for the woods. I climbed onto the wall and walked along its edge, hoping to catch a closer glimpse of the doe. At that, she scampered away. Twigs snapped under her hooves. Then she was gone.

"*Pssst.* Hey, Dee!" Web leaned back on the hind legs of her chair, which was pulled up to a small study table in the school library. With one hand, she kept a firm grip on the table's edge to balance herself; with the other, she waved me over to join her. I squirmed free of my knapsack to sit in the chair next to Web.

"Why didn't you call me back?" she asked.

After I'd gotten Web's message, my mind had turned to other things—Lorelle's letter, and the situation with Lindsay at school. "I meant to call, Web," I said, wondering if I should tell her about Lindsay. "But see, something went down with my sister at home that made me forget to call."

"Well anyway, how'd the pictures come out, the ones from lacrosse tryouts?"

"I won't know till later, when my mom takes me to pick them up at Print Works."

Web said, "You been thinking any more about 'sembly? That's why I called."

"Look, Web, taking pictures is one thing; entering them in a contest is another."

"C'mon, Dee. You could enter the shot of me with my lacrosse stick. It'll be a tribute to my lacrosse days, which are *over*. I'm done with that game, Dee. *Done*."

"You and me both," I said. I looked for a place to unload the books in my knapsack, but Web's stuff cluttered everything. Colored markers, a plastic mirror, books, two packs of Day-Glo Mango gum, and a pair of hoop earrings littered the table. Web's sweater was draped over the back of the only free chair, and her shoes rested on the chair's seat.

"You see this?" Web held up Ledbetter's *Pre-Algebra*. "This book could cure insomnia; it's so big, you could use it to throw at muggers—if Wexford *had* any muggers," she said, laughing.

Stacy Snead and some other girls at the next table watched

me and Web. They snatched careful glances. I shrugged, think-ing about those mean girls at Lindsay's school. I wondered if Kippy Tate, the lacrosse girl from Green Crest, knew Stacy Snead, the lacrosse girl from Wexford Middle. Stacy and I ex-changed a quick once-over. Then she whispered something to her friends, while pointing at Web.

Web said, "Stacy wants to know what *I'm* doing here with *you*. She's scared of you."

I slid my eyes in Stacy's direction. "*Scared* of me? I've had people mad at me, sick of me, even in love with me, but never scared of me," I said. "You're making that up."

"Making it up, nothing. After Stacy saw me sitting with you at tryouts, she told me the all-time stupidest thing I ever heard—told me to be careful."

"Careful of what?"

"Careful of you, Dee," Web said with a stunted laugh, the kind of laugh when you can't believe something's really true. "Careful of you and your family," she went on. "Stacy said you could be trouble." Web was shaking her head, flinging an angry version of her smirk at Stacy's table.

I shifted my chair and tried to blink back the numbness that was filling me up fast. "Careful of *me*—and my *family*?" I wanted to make sure I was hearing Web right.

Web nodded. "That's what Miss Ball-and-Stick said."

Stacy and her friends were watching me. When I looked to-ward their table a second time, they pretended to be busy with their schoolwork. I wasn't going to give them the satisfaction of messing up any more of the time I was spending with Web. The whole thing *was* the stupidest trash I'd ever heard. And all of it deserved a stupid comeback. I slid my chair closer to Web, so my back faced Stacy's table. With my hand on my hip, I said to

Web, "Right. You *better* be careful. Before we moved here, my dad took out a map and pointed to Wexford. He looked at my sister and my mom and me and said, 'Let's ruin Wexford, Connecticut. Let's pack up everything this minute and move to *Wexford, Connecticut,* so we can make a whole bunch of white folks miserable—and scared!'"

Web did her smirk, the funny one that I was coming to know. She could tell I was kidding. "Cute," she said.

"Cute, schmute. I'm telling the truth, Web. I couldn't wait to move away from all my friends to come to Wexford to make kids nervous. But Web, you're messing up my plan. It's not working on you. I'm starting to *like* you." A giggle found its way up and out.

"It's weird, Dee. When I lived in Queens, some of the white kids talked about the black kids like they were dogs. They said stuff like, 'Watch your back around a black.'" Web kept her balance while she tilted back in her chair. "Here, nobody ever talks about black kids, probably because there aren't any—well, there *weren't* any.

"Two years ago, though, there *was* another black family who moved to Wexford. One of the kids, Kendra, was in my school, Wexford Elementary, but not in my grade. Kids used to watch her all the time too. Her and her brother, Danny, who was older." I was listening to Web real close; I didn't know another black family had lived in Wexford before us.

"Where are they now?" I asked.

"After summer vacation, Kendra and Danny didn't come back to school. People said the family had moved away, almost as fast as they came. I guess they didn't like Wexford...." Web lowered her eyes.

"Or Wexford didn't like *them,*" I said.

Web nodded. "Dee, when you showed up in Mr. McCurdy's class on your first day, kids started talking," she explained. "It's the same thing that happened when that girl Kendra and her brother came to school."

With my chair faced away, I couldn't see Stacy and her friends, but the weight of their watchful eyes pressed at my back. "That's how it was in my neighborhood back home in Baltimore," I said. "A lot of black kids talking down white kids." I sighed.

"You ever talk mean about whites, Dee?"

No one had ever asked me that before. Until then, I hadn't really thought about it. But almost everybody I knew had something nasty to say about white folks. I played with the zipper on my knapsack so I didn't have to look right at Web. "You ever say mean things about blacks?" I asked.

"I asked you first," Web said.

"I asked you second, and two's a higher number."

"C'mon Dee. Be brave. *Stacy's* scared of you, I'm not."

I had a million mean things I'd said about white people at one time or another. But I couldn't say them to Web. Web wasn't white *people*. Web was *Web*. I shrugged. "This is dumb. I'm not doing it," I said.

"Okay, suit yourself. You had your chance to put down a white girl, right to her face." Web flipped her wrist to check the time on a make-believe watch. "C'mon, I'll give you ten seconds. Speak now, or you'll lose your chance. Ten... nine...eight..."

"You're out of your mind, Web, you know that. Why don't you let yourself fall back in that chair so you can knock some sense into your silly head." I folded my arms and copied Web's smirk.

"Three...two...one...." Web let go of the table's edge and landed, sitting straight in her chair. "Time's up," she said.

"What about you?" I asked.

"What *about* me?" Web played with her hair.

"What mean thing did you say about a black person?" I asked.

"Don't you remember? You were sitting right there, and whew, you sure looked mad."

I raised an eyebrow. "*You* said something racist about *me*?"

"It was in Mr. McCurdy's class, when we were talking about American poets. You named Langston Hughes. And I said, 'Langston *who*?'"

I laughed and shook my head. "Web, that wasn't racist, just stupid."

Web pushed her bangs away from her face. "Seems to me they're the same thing."

That night, I wrote back to Lorelle. The yellowy light shining from my bedroom desk lamp made the blue lines on my notebook look green. I printed as neat as I could.

Dear Lorelle,

I tried out for the girls' lacrosse team. Everybody here plays lacrosse. Lacrosse is kind of like stickball, except the stick has a net pouch on the end. It's kind of hard to explain. But it doesn't matter. I didn't make the team.

My school, Wexford Middle School, is like you said—a bunch of white kids. I got a good English teacher, Mr. McCurdy. Lorelle, this man is crusty-old. Like he's gonna go any minute. All the kids talk mean about him because he's a fright to look at, like Mr. Buford, who lives on Packard Street.

But Lorelle, Mr. McCurdy knew Langston Hughes. He told me about it one day.

The ink in my pen was fading. I took a new pen from the jelly jar on my desk. Before I went on with my letter, I read it from the beginning.

> I met a girl named Web (it's a nickname) who used to live in Queens, in New York City. She's not like the other kids here. Well, she's white, but not white like we know. She doesn't get uptight around black people, at least not around me.
>
> Web can't double-dutch. See, none of the kids here double-dutch. There's not really a corner where everybody hangs out. It's more like long streets with trees. I keep getting hay fever, which makes me sneeze, especially when I'm nervous or upset.
>
> Lorelle, with this letter I'm sending a copy of a picture of a doe I saw in the woods near my street. Bambi lives in my neighborhood (ha! ha!), and she's the only neighbor I've met so far! People here don't greet on the avenue (actually, there aren't any avenues). I also put in a picture of a girl named Stacy Snead playing lacrosse. Stacy plays lacrosse as good as you and I double-dutch. I took her picture at tryouts so you could see what lacrosse looks like.

I set down my pen and shook the writer's cramp from my hand. Sifting through the batch of photos from my day at the lacrosse field, I came to the shot of Web blowing her Banana Bubble. Then I found a picture of Web posing with her lacrosse stick, holding it like a guitar. I thought about including the pictures of Web with my letter, but when I sorted through them again, Web looked too silly to be my friend.

I imagined Lorelle and Rhonda sitting on Lorelle's front stoop, cracking up at Web's picture, making all kinds of white-girl jokes. If I'd been sitting there with them and someone else had sent my letter, I'd probably be laughing along. Lorelle and I were always talking about white kids being prejudiced, but I guess we were sort of prejudiced too. I took off my glasses to clean the lenses with my shirttail, wondering how to end my letter.

> Some of the kids at my school are afraid of me. Most of the girls at Wexford Middle School don't even know my name. But they're scared of me anyhow, thinking be-cause I'm black, I'm gonna make some kind of problem.

I stopped writing for a minute, remembering the afternoon I'd spent in the library with Web.

> It makes me all angry inside. Like a red fire, just burn-ing. Sometimes it makes me want to cry. Lorelle, one day I asked myself, What did I ever do to make people think I'm wicked? When I thought about it, I couldn't find an answer. I also wonder if moving to Wexford was the right thing. When my daddy got his new job, he thought the move was a good idea. Maybe it's a good idea gone bad.

I had already written four pages. I had so much to tell Lorelle. My writing hand couldn't keep up with everything coming into my head at once. I also wanted to tell Lorelle about Lindsay, and about Mom and Dad's argument. But I couldn't put that down. It was all too much.

I looked over the letter Lorelle had sent me, trying to re-member what else I needed to tell her.

Lorelle, I think you should keep your hair the way it is. You've got the prettiest hair in the neighborhood, curly and soft like the nubby fur collar on your aunt Vonette's winter coat. Remember, we agreed to keep our hair nat-ural. We hooked our pinkies and shook on it. We made our deal solid—natural hair or nothing. Perms are for up-pity kids who want straight hair like a game-show lady's. If you *do* get a perm, Lorelle, I'll still be your friend, but send me a picture so I can see how straight hair looks on you. It's hard to picture you looking any different.

Congratulations on getting your period. I'm still pray-ing for mine. Whenever I ask Mom about it, she says, "Pu-berty takes patience." When I tell her I'm sick of waiting, she says, "Patience is a virtue."

Sometimes I think mothers have a secret club where they sit around and make up stuff to tell their kids (smile).

Say hi to your mama and Aunt Vonette for me, and write back soon.

Love,
Dee

I read my letter over, making sure all the spelling was right. Before I folded it into its envelope, I added:

P.S. Your new jump, Groove Move, sounds hard. I hope you get to go to Washington, D.C. They got a thing here at school called the Founders' Day Assembly. It's a talent contest. That girl I told you about, Web, keeps trying to get me to enter it with my pictures. Instead, I wish I could enter it with the Jumpin' Jive Five, so we could show everybody how we jump.

I moved on to a fifth sheet of notebook paper. I didn't want to say good-bye to Lorelle.

P.P.S. I asked my mom if I could visit this summer. She said, "We'll see." (That's what I mean about mothers.)

One last thought, and then I could end my letter.

P.P.P.S. How's Rhonda working out as a Jumpin' Jive Five?

9

I woke up to Lindsay's moaning. "*Mom.* It's my tummy—grinding, and queasy, like something's grubbing on my insides!" It was two days after Lindsay had told me about those girls at Green Crest. Now, from my bedroom, I could hear her begging Mom to let her stay home from school.

"Show me where it hurts," Mom was saying. I rolled over under my covers and listened. Lindsay said, "If I go to school, I'll throw up—all over."

Mom told Linds to rest. "Could be a bug," Mom said. "A day in bed will do you good."

And that was that.

But after school, while I helped Mom sweep the kitchen, she said, "Lindsay's been quiet all day. I think her tummy ache is a cover-up for something else, don't you?" Mom studied me for a long moment.

"I don't know," I said, then I looked down at the broom bristles and didn't take my eyes away from the tiles on the floor. I swept every last crumb and crevice.

Mom could smell a secret a million miles away. I thought, All I have to do is catch her eye for a second, and she'll know I'm hiding something. "Linds'll get better" was the only other thing I could think of to say.

What I knew of Lindsay's trouble at Green Crest was a burden, weighing heavy on my nerves. I suspected Kippy Tate was the reason Lindsay was sick, and I wanted to tell Mom about the whole thing. But Linds and me, we'd done the Redmond Avenue pinky shake. And that meant no giving her secret away, no matter what.

That night, Dad came home from work before dark. I'd driven with Mom to pick up Dad at the train station, hoping to get some shots of the sunset. At Mom's urging, Lindsay had come along too. "The fresh air will do you—and your tummy—some good," Mom had said.

The Wexford station was no more than a clapboard structure with tracks out back. Mom called it rustic; I called it rickety. Lindsay wasn't saying much of anything. An American flag—a little one on a stick—hung over the station door. It wrinkled in the warm May breeze.

Mom and Lindsay and I sat in the car, waiting for Dad's train to arrive, the Danbury Line that was bringing him home from Grand Central Station, in New York City. Lindsay sat quietly, watching out the window. Her elbow was dug into her thigh; her chin rested on her palm. A frown pinched the skin on her forehead. I stretched my head and shoulders out the car window to focus on the spiky weeds that poked up between the railroad ties.

Ch-click...ch-click...

In the distance, I heard the train's engine. And soon its

headlights grew brighter and closer. As the Danbury Line raced toward the station, the weeds on the tracks leaned away—hard, as if they were scared of what was coming. The train slowed, hissed, then rolled to a creaky stop. Behind the train's club car, the sun hung low on the horizon. It made a hot-copper background for the sleek silver train. *Ch-click...*

Men whose gray suits all looked the same got off the train. They gathered in little groups. Some shared rides home. Others joked about the heat and gave each other friendly slaps on the back. Those men stuck together, the same way Stacy and her friends did. Dad was dressed like the rest of them, but he stepped down from the train alone. His trench coat was thrown over his arm. The polished leather on his briefcase matched his shoes. *Ch-click...ch-click...*

As I snapped the shutter, I wondered if those white men ever gave Dad a hard time, the way Stacy did to me—or if they ever messed with Dad, the way Kippy Tate and her friends had picked on Lindsay.

Dad stood next to the phone booth, looking for our car. Mom pumped the car horn. "Bennett, honey," she shouted, "over here!" When Dad saw us, his face brightened with a smile. He waved, then came to the car.

"Hey, hey," he said, "tonight I got the royal pickup—met by my queen and my two lovely ladies. Makes me feel like a king." Dad stuck his head in the open car window to kiss Mom. He took a second look in the backseat, where Lindsay and I sat. Gently lifting Lindsay's chin, he asked, "How's my sickly princess?"

"Still sickly" was all Lindsay said.

Lindsay and I exchanged a quick glance while Dad went around to the driver's side of the car. Mom slid over on the front seat to let Dad drive. She said, "Well, look here. *Brown* sugar behind the wheel of a *blue* car—and home from work early!"

Dad kissed Mom again. He raised his face to look at me and Lindsay in the rearview mirror. A glimmer of sunset flickered in Dad's eyes, along with a relaxed expression that I'd forgotten Dad's eyes ever had. The sun highlighted the brown hairs in his mustache. He said, "Work ain't all there is, lady love."

We were stopped at a yield sign, waiting to drive over Township Crossing, a one-way drawbridge that crossed a stream next to the Wexford train station. A police car drove toward us, crossing the bridge from the other side. When the policeman passed us on the road, he nodded and tipped his cap. "Dad," I asked, "you ever get messed with? Bothered by white people, I mean?"

My eyes met Dad's in the rearview mirror. Mom inclined her head toward me in the backseat. Dad didn't answer right away. Then he said, "I'm afraid I do…. You see, there's a security guard at work who's had his eye on me since I've come to Kentwood." Lindsay turned her attention from watching out the window to looking at Dad. I felt her shift next to me on the seat.

"That guard, he still bother you?" I asked.

Mom said, "Dee, your father's had a long day. Let him clear his mind."

"It's okay, Grace, it's okay," Dad said, calm and low. "These days, my mind's as clear as it's ever been. Everything's clear to me, Grace. Everything." When we drove over Township Crossing, Dad flicked on his turn signal and made a left onto Clover Drive, where, farther along the winding road, sat the Wexford Middle School. Dad loosened the knot in his tie. "That guard bothers *himself*," he said. "And, as much as I hate to admit it, *he's* troubled *me* for a while—he's yanked on my nerves one too many times with his mind games and power plays."

Lindsay leaned over the back of Dad's seat. "What kind of mind games?" she asked.

"And what kind of power plays?" I wanted to know.

"Girls, let your father drive in peace."

"Grace, they've got to learn."

Mom slid on her sunglasses. Now *she* was looking out the window. "I suppose they do," she said with a sigh.

I could see Wexford Middle School up ahead. When we passed Manley Field, Dad said, "That guard's curious. He wants to know how a black man has a big office at Kentwood Corporation. And boy, a few weeks back he got crazy with wondering. He went off the deep end and almost took me with him."

Mom rushed in, as if she didn't want Dad to finish. "Bennett, this is not the time to—"

"When *is* the time, Grace?"

"I just don't think we have to discuss this right now."

"They need to know, Grace."

Lindsay sat back on the seat, away from Mom and Dad's tense words. They were speaking to each other like they'd done on that rainy night. And, like that night, the same trembly shudder shook me from the inside out.

Mom went back to staring out the window. She folded her arms. Manley Field grew smaller in the distance. Dad picked up where he'd left off. "I'd only been at Kentwood for a few weeks. I was in my office, working late," he began. "It might have been around eight-thirty. When I was leaving—going to the elevator—the building security guard stopped me."

As Dad told his story, I gripped the strap of my camera case tight in my fist. I glanced over at Lindsay, whose eyes had grown wide with listening. I could almost feel Mom's face twisting into a frown. Dad sighed, then went on. "'Who let you in here?' the guard asked me. I told him I *worked* at Kentwood. I said I recently came on board, 'vice president of special sales—bottling division'—that's what I told him," Dad explained.

For a moment we drove in silence, dusk creeping in around our car. I thought back to the patches of argument I'd over-heard between Mom and Dad. Now Dad's story was filling in the gaps. He said, "Then that guard backed me up in a corner."

I heard Mom draw in a harsh breath. Dad shook his head, then spoke as if he was talking to himself, still working things through in his mind. He said, "I'm standing there in my suit and tie, I've got my briefcase in my hand, and this man has got my back to the wall."

Lindsay leaned forward again. I couldn't help but join her. "What'd he do?" she asked.

"What'd *you* do?" I asked.

"I slipped my hand in my breast pocket, reached into my wallet, and pulled out my Kentwood corporate ID card—put it on the desk in front of me," Dad said. "After I showed him my Kentwood card, all that guard could say was, 'Make sure you turn off the lights when you leave.'"

We were driving along Hunter Road now, past the Wexford Riding Academy, which sent the smell of hay and horses into our car. "Showing him your ID put him in his place?" Lindsay asked.

Dad shook his head. "Not quite. He tried another power play on me today. But I wasn't letting him get away with it."

Mom looked over the top of her sunglasses. *"Again?"* she asked, an alarmed expression growing in her eyes. I licked my lips. They'd grown dry, probably from taking long breaths with my mouth hanging open.

"Yes, Grace, again. But you can bet that after today it'll be *never* again," Dad said. "See, when I came to the office this morning, I got off the elevator with Rob Callahan, who works over in the promotions department. That guard watched both me and Rob come in the front entrance. Rob cut left, toward his office, no problem. But me, he stopped me, just beyond the reception area. It was early, seven-thirty maybe. Some of the lights were still turned off. And there he was, flinging me a sneer. 'I'll need to see your ID. House policy,' he says."

"He was working a triple power play," Lindsay said.

"And a double-triple mind game," I added.

While watching the road, Dad tilted his head toward us to tell us the rest of the story. "I held my ID card out in front of him, stepped up to that guy, and said, 'We've done this dance before. You've seen me. You've seen my ID. Look at me. Take a *good look* at my face, man. I'm not a stranger. Kentwood is my employer. I work here. I *belong* here. Just like you. I'm not going to let you stand there and intimidate me.'"

"Amen to that, Bennett," Mom said.

"Amen times ten!" I said, a proud smile stretching across my face.

"You've always stood your ground, Bennett," Mom said.

Dad finished his story. "So the guard's blinking real fast—and squirming. He says to me, 'I'm just doing my job.'

"That's when I said to him, 'Fine, do your job. But respect me, man.' And before he could speak another word, Callahan came around the corner, saying, 'You all right, Willis?'"

I could feel my proud smile starting to spread all over my body, replacing the rattly feeling brought on by Mom and Dad's spat. Lindsay looked as if she was mulling it all over, nodding and listening when Dad spoke. "Then," Dad went on, "quick and measly, the guard says, 'Didn't mean no harm.' And, Grace, that was the best I could hope for."

Mom reached over and brushed Dad's cheek with the back of her hand. "You've been through a lot, Bennett," she said.

Dad sighed. He looked at Mom, then into the rearview mirror at me and Linds. "*You've* been through a lot with *me*."

"That guard did you wrong," I said.

"He took a piece of my integrity," Dad admitted.

"But you got it back," Lindsay said.

The road ahead was straight and narrow, with heavy-branched trees on each side. "Yeah, but you can bet that guy's still got me on his mind. He and some of the other men at Kentwood—executives like me—can't help but watch me like a slow-to-boil teakettle."

"That's what happens to me at school," I said, "kids *watching* me, wondering about me—and scared of me, without even knowing me. There's one girl, Stacy Snead, she's the worst."

"Some white people can be funny that way," Dad said. "But it's nothing new, Dee, girl. The men at Kentwood who eyeball me when I'm coming out of a meeting in the chairman's office or standing in line with them at the coffee wagon are just like the boys who used to check me out when I had my newspaper route in Colesville, when I was ten. The white boys who lived on the other side of town—that's where I delivered my papers—eagle-eyed me all the time, coming and going. They didn't see many black boys and girls in their neighborhood. And the way they looked at me, you would've thought I had two heads."

We were driving along Acorn Road, the road that led to Scarlet Oak, and home.

"When I first went to Wexford Middle, they looked at me like I didn't have a head at all," I said.

Dad flipped down the sun visor to shade his window from the blurred ball of sun setting in front of us. "Now *that's* a shame, as pretty as you are," he said.

Lindsay had leaned back in the seat. She sat real still, listening to me and Dad.

"I guess we both—we all—got it hard, you being the only black man at work, me—well, me and Linds—being new black girls at our schools." Behind me, I heard Lindsay let out a quiet sigh.

"Dad," I said slowly, "sometimes I think moving to Wexford was a bad idea."

Dad shook his head. "I'd be lying if I said I didn't have that thought from time to time—especially when bad stuff goes down at the office." Our eyes met again in the rearview mirror. Now Dad's expression was clouded with regret. "And I was so wrapped up in all my big dreams—work, commuting, making it—that I didn't take time to consider all that you, Linds, and your mom were going through."

We drove in silence for a moment. Then Dad said, "I'm sorry the road's been so hard for you, Dee. It's been tough on me too—tough on all of us." I nodded a slow single nod. Dad said, "When it gets to be too much, I try to remember that even though I'm the only black vice president at Kentwood, I'm *not* the only black man who works hard and wants nice things for his family—or the only black person who's trying to prove himself in a white man's world."

"You got *that* right," Linds said, almost too soft to hear.

"When I'm at work, when fear and loneliness snatch me up, I close the door to my office and have a little conversation with myself. I say, Bennett, you've got three things going for you: You have a wonderful family. You're qualified to do your job. And you're black."

Dad's eyes were thoughtful as he watched the road. "What do you do when people stare?" I asked.

"There's a good way to deal with people looking. It's something that I learned when I was a boy, when I couldn't get through a day of delivering papers without the eyes of ignorance watching my every move."

Mom had gone back to peering out the window. In her side mirror, I could see the reflection of the setting sun and the trees dancing on the glare of her sunglasses. Dad said, "When white folks stare and wonder and show disrespect, it's best to kindly— but firmly—let them know that you won't stand for it. Then you've just got to go on about your business. I figure if they don't have anything better to do than watch every blink I make, then boo-*hoo* for *them*."

Dad winked at me and Lindsay in the rearview mirror. "Or maybe we should just say *boo*—right *to* them. That would truly give them something to be scared of." I laughed with Dad. In the side mirror, I could see Mom smiling.

She said, "You two are two berries from the same silly pie."

I slid back in the seat, next to Lindsay. Her lips were wearing a little smile too. When we passed Morning Glory Circle, I knew we'd be home soon. Scarlet Oak was a few minutes away.

The sun had slipped behind a fence of evergreens, leaving a dim crimson sky. Dad turned on his headlights. Scarlet Oak loomed into view.

As we wheeled down our driveway, I wondered what would happen if I said *boo* right *to* Stacy Snead.

10

That night, Lindsay didn't eat much for dinner, so I took a tray of food to her bedroom. "I brought you some chicken-noodle soup," I said. "And raisin toast—burnt around the crust, like you like it." Lindsay was playing with Bacon, staring past me.

"Linds," I asked slowly, "you really got a stomachache?"

Lindsay shook her head. She slid her eyes sideways to look at me. "Uh-uh, Dee, my stomach *doesn't* hurt. It's just that...I can't face Kippy and them till I figure out what to do about the way they treated me."

"You could do what Dad did—tell them you're not taking it anymore."

With a single nod, Lindsay said, "Dad spoke his mind all right. He handled that guard head-on." Lindsay pulled Bacon's tail. "Yeah, Dad got me to thinking *hard,*" she said. "But now, Dee, I gotta find the right way for *me* to speak *my* mind."

We sat silent for a moment. Lindsay's expression bent into a little frown, as if she was puzzled about something. She took a bite of toast. "You know something, Dee? When I'm out there on the field playing lacrosse, I forget all about Kippy Tate and her mean friends. Sometimes when I'm cradling, I don't even remember where I am. Wexford is a million miles away. All I feel are my legs pushing and my heart pumping—fast, like I'm flying, like nothing else matters."

I nodded agreement. "I used to feel that way when I jumped with the Jive Five." I curled my feet up under me on the bed. "And I think that's what Daddy felt when he told that security guard to stop his mess," I said.

Lindsay shrugged. "Yeah, I guess he felt like he'd won at something."

With my finger, I traced the flower pattern on Lindsay's comforter. "You can't play lacrosse from this bed," I said. "While you're sitting here, Kippy Tate is making points. And the last thing she and her evil friends are thinking about is Lindsay Willis's stomachache."

Lindsay took a taste of soup. Then she ate the rest of her toast, crust first. I sighed. "It's hard for me to keep your secret, Linds. Mom knows something's up."

Toast crumbs stuck to the corners of Lindsay's mouth. She said, "How many points you think Kippy could score in the day I've been gone?"

"There's only one way to find that out," I said.

After school a week later, the school bus dropped me off, like always. I grabbed the mail from the mailbox and started to walk toward the house.

But the mail made me stop.

There was the latest issue of *Photo World* magazine (the subscription people finally got my change-of-address form) and a letter from Lorelle!

Lorelle had written to me on the kind of stationery that is

paper and envelope all in one. The letter folded over itself to make a perfect square. A wax stamp sealed the edges. On the front, up by the postmark, it said JIVE FIVE UPDATE. PRIVATE! I held the pink envelope up to the sun. Through it I could make out a few words written in purple ink—*fights, bad, Rhonda*. A woman, speeding on a motorcycle in the desert, raced across *Photo World*'s cover. Near her picture, the cover line promised 20 TIPS FOR GREAT ACTION SHOTS.

I didn't know which to read first—Lorelle's letter or the article on taking action pictures. I could hardly wait to read them both. But Lorelle was my *girl*. And to me, a private Jive Five update meant I should read her letter right away.

I shimmied my knapsack off my back, then tucked my magazine inside. I tied the sleeves of my jacket around my waist. Carefully, I peeled open the edges of Lorelle's letter.

Dee,

I need to write this quick. I got a report due tomorrow for Mrs. Williamson's class. Remember her? She doesn't take no excuses. She told me I had to keep getting B's so she could go on bragging about me at her teacher meetings.

But Dee, stuff is happening! First, Mama took me to Trudy's Salon, down on Stedwick Boulevard, to get a perm. I wanted to get my hair done for a big picnic next week in Community Park.

Anyway, when I got in the chair, Miss Trudy's daughter, Althea (that girl with the pretty complexion and long fingernails), put a smock over me. She had everything set up. The hair grease, the perm kit, the plastic gloves, and the comb.

But when Althea went off to answer the phone at the

front of the shop, I started thinking about your letter and realized you were right. My natural hair does look prettier than most girls' on the block. I sat in that salon chair getting second thoughts on top of second thoughts. What if my hair never grew back to how it was? I was scared, Dee. Before Althea came back, I jumped up and threw off the smock. I grabbed my jacket and books. I told Mama to forget the whole thing.

So I'm keeping my hair natural. That's part of the news. But the Jive Five update I wanted to write and tell you about is Rhonda. Dee, Rhonda's been getting in more fights. Bad fights! She got expelled from school for a week. When I went over to her house to see her, she looked bad, Dee. Like somebody had smacked her good. I told her people wouldn't mess with her if she didn't start in with her loud talk and shoving.

I told her she couldn't jump with the Jive Five anymore if she kept it up. Then she started to pick a fight with *me*. She said the Jive Five was nothing, and that I couldn't kick her off the team, because she was quitting.

That was last week. I haven't seen or heard from Rhonda since then. Rhonda scared me, Dee. She would've beat me right there on her stoop if her mama hadn't called her back in the house. Anyway, now we're down to four jumpers. We need you back, Dee. Jumping with four isn't the same. Are you coming this summer?

If you don't come, I don't know if we'll be able to jump in Street Fest this year. That means we wouldn't have a chance to go to Washington, D.C. You're the only one we could teach to do Groove Move in time.

Well, it's going on ten o'clock (at night), so I better

end it here. Mama and Aunt Vonette think I'm in bed asleep. Actually, I *am* in bed, but I got my notebook spread open and a flashlight on so I can finish my paper.

Thanks for the pictures you sent. Lacrosse looks hard. But your picture taking is starting to look professional. Tell Linds I said what's up.

Love,
Lorelle

While I finished Lorelle's letter, my lower lip got heavy. My mouth fell open. I started to read the letter again from the beginning, but before I could get past the first sentence, my eyes darted down the page. Those purple words jumped up in front of me like monsters: *Rhonda...bad fights...expelled from school...smacked her good...loud talk and shoving...scared me, Dee...* I closed my mouth to swallow. Without taking another look at the letter, I folded it into a square so small, it fit inside the spare-change pocket of my knapsack. I made sure the letter was tucked beneath a wad of Kleenex and my leftover lunch money. Then I hoisted my knapsack onto one shoulder.

My shoes crunched the driveway gravel in a soft, steady rhythm. I walked real slow, not wanting to go into the house right away. Mom would ask me about my day. And after reading Lorelle's letter, I wasn't sure how my day was.

I took smaller, slower steps toward the house. Inside my shoes, my socks stuck to my feet. I couldn't tell Mom about Rhonda. If she knew, she'd never let me spend the summer with Lorelle.

I stood outside on the back porch before going into the kitchen. I studied the pattern on our braided doorway mat.

WELCOME was woven in red. For a minute, I thought about inviting Lorelle to spend the summer with me in Wexford. She could sleep on a cot in my room.

But what would me and Lorelle do in *Wexford*? We couldn't double-dutch, not with just the two of us. Nobody could twirl ropes like the other girls in the Jive Five. We needed the whole team. But they *all* couldn't come to Connecticut. Besides, even though the Jive Five was down to four, I knew Lorelle wouldn't want to miss Street Fest and her chance to jump in the double-dutch championship in Washington, D.C.

And compared with Baltimore, Connecticut had nothing happening. Wexford didn't have a corner store that sold chocolate-flavored licorice sticks. There weren't any ice-cream trucks that gave away free Popsicles on Sundays. And even though I never asked, I was sure the people on Scarlet Oak Lane didn't get together on summer nights to play music and dance in the street.

Before I went into the house, I checked my knapsack's change pocket. I wanted to make sure I'd buried Lorelle's letter deep down inside.

Lately, Dad had come home in time for dinner every night. He said working late was a thing of the past.

Lindsay was back in school and talking like her old self again. "Passalt," she said, crunching on an ear of corn.

"It's *pass the salt*," Mom corrected, looking pleased to see Lindsay eating again.

"Gebba Willis used to say *passalt*, two words made into one," Lindsay said.

"All right, but eat slower so that you don't put indigestion—and another ache—onto your stomach," Mom warned.

I was starved and going to town on a biscuit.

Dad's eyes were playful. He said, "Dinner tastes better when I'm sharing it with my ladies, for a change—*passalt.*" Dad winked at Linds.

"Passpepper," I said, grabbing my own piece of corn.

"All right, you three," Mom said. For a minute, we all ate like there was no tomorrow, passing the platter of meat, adding gravy to our potatoes, and buttering our bread. When I looked up from my plate, I saw Mom steal a cautious glimpse at Lindsay. "Linds, sweetheart, I got a call from your lacrosse coach today," she said.

Lindsay didn't look up. She kept crunching on her corn. "Uh-huh."

"Your coach said you wouldn't play at practice." I turned my eyes in Lindsay's direction. Linds had stopped chewing. She and Mom were locked in a loaded look.

"The coach said you *refused* to play."

Lindsay put down her corn. "That's right. I *did* refuse." Dad wiped his mouth with his napkin and gave Lindsay all his attention. "I *wouldn't* play." Lindsay said it slow, as if she was remembering. My eyes shot from Lindsay to Mom to Dad, then back to Lindsay. Mom spooned potatoes onto Lindsay's plate.

"Was your stomach acting up again?" Mom asked.

"No," Lindsay said quietly, "it wasn't my stomach. It was never my stomach.... I *was* hurt, though. But I'm not hurt now. I'm better."

Lindsay started to say something else but didn't. For a moment, the only sound at our dinner table was the clanking of our silverware. In the midst of our silent, careful eating, Lindsay spoke. "Some girls at school did me wrong," she said softly. I placed my hand on Lindsay's leg under the table to let her know it was okay to talk about it.

Her shoulders curled in, folding up around her ears. She told Mom and Dad everything. When she explained about those mean girls at Green Crest, Dad's face tightened and Mom's eyes filled with concern. Mom said, "Lord, have mercy."

Dad, who looked like he was eager to hear more, touched Mom's shoulder and said gently, "Let her finish, Grace. Let her speak."

That's when Linds told the rest of her story, the part about pretending she was white. She forced her eyes onto the napkin in her lap and twisted her fingers around each other. When she was finished, a big breath of relief escaped from her chest. *"Whew!"*

I blew out a breath too, and felt a bundle of worry tumble off my back. But Lindsay had more to say. "I told my coach what'd happened that day in the locker room," she went on, "and that I wouldn't play lacrosse until Kippy and her friends apologized to me. I told the coach all I want is what's owed me—for them to say they're sorry."

I gave Lindsay's thigh a little squeeze. She said, "I wouldn't—*couldn't*—score any more points on a team where some of my own teammates treated me trashy." Mom and Dad were listening hard. "Kippy and them, they *did* apologize." Lindsay looked at Mom, then Dad.

"But you know what?" she said.

Dad said, "Speak on it, child."

"Even if they hadn't said they were sorry, the point is, I let them know I wasn't taking no junk from nobody no more."

Dad and Mom exchanged a glance. "How you feeling now?" Mom asked.

"My hurting's gone," Lindsay said. Then, clear and straight, she added, "Acting white got me as far as a car gets with no gas."

"Linds, that's the *truth*," I said. Under the table, I hooked my pinky to Lindsay's, and we shook and shook and shook.

The following week, announcements for the Founders' Day Assembly hung everywhere at school. There were flyers in each classroom, on the doors and walls and bulletin boards; a Founders' Day banner decorated the cafeteria, done up in red, white, and blue. After Mr. McCurdy's class, Web stopped me in the hall. "Dee," she said, "'sembly's soon, you know—and like I been saying, it's big in Wexford. Real big."

"Like lacrosse," I said.

"Like lacrosse—but different. See, you—well, we—stink at lacrosse, but you could really show your stuff at 'sembly, Dee."

I leaned on the wall near the lockers. The cold cinder blocks chilled my back and shoulders. I let Web talk. "Stacy Snead," she said, her smirk starting up on her face. "You still got the pictures you took of Stacy on Manley Field, cradling during lacrosse tryouts?"

"They're at home with the rest of my pictures. But what's *that* got to do with—"

"Because the only thing Stacy loves more than playing lacrosse is *pictures* of her playing lacrosse—anything that shows off how good she is with her stick."

I couldn't follow Web's thinking. "C'mon, Web, talk straight. You're supposed to be twisting my arm about this Assembly thing."

Web's smirk turned to a grin, as if she was holding on to a good idea. "I'm getting to all that," she said. The hall was growing empty. Everybody was rushing to class. Web swung her arm around my shoulders. "Where you walking to?" she asked.

"Mr. Clem's class—Social Studies," I said.

"C'mon, I'm going to Mr. Lafayette's room, two doors down from Clem. The bell's gonna ring any minute. We'll walk and talk at the same time."

On the way, Web tried one last time to convince me to enter the Founders' Day Assembly. As we walked, the class bell rang, and soon Web and I were the only ones in the hallway. Web led me to a drinking fountain in the corner, where we'd be out of sight.

I shrugged. "I don't know, Web."

"Dee, c'mon. Your pictures can't be any less of a talent than what other kids have done in the past. Last year, this girl got up on stage and showed everybody how to iron clothes. She wore a leotard, and lipstick."

"Yeah, right. Who would do something like that?"

Web unwrapped a piece of gum and pushed it into her mouth. "*I* would," she said.

I giggled. "*You* would."

"Listen, Dee, it's like I told you before. Last year, Stacy Snead won 'sembly with her lacrosse stick. I bet your photos show a hundred *times* more talent. And if you exhibit your pictures, Stacy'll think twice about telling kids to be careful of you." I was starting to think Web was onto something. "Besides," she said, "what've you got to lose?"

Web was right. I didn't have a thing to lose. What I *did* have were some half-decent photos that I'd taken since I'd come to Wexford. "Okay, I'll do it," I said.

"*Yes!* Camera Dee takes on 'sembly!" Web bumped her hip to mine.

While Web and I walked to the end of the hall, where the doors to our classrooms were closed, I tried to come up with an excuse for being late. Web must have been thinking the same thing. She stopped a few classrooms away from Mr. Clem's and said, "Tell him you had a female problem and couldn't figure out how to use the sanitary dispenser in the girls' room. Guy teachers never ask for more of an explanation than that."

I promised Web I'd gather up my best pictures and enter them in the Founders' Day Assembly. But before I turned to go, Web said, "Oh, Dee, there's one more thing. In your photo exhibit, make sure you include one of the pictures you took of Stacy Snead scoring on Manley Field. Blow it up real big."

I squinted my face into a frown. Stacy Snead was the last person I wanted in my exhibit. I thought Web was making a joke, until, stone serious, she said, "As last year's 'sembly winner, Stacy is this year's contest judge."

After last period, I signed up for the Founders' Day Assembly. A contest enrollment sheet hung from a clipboard next to the auditorium stage. Before writing my name, I gave my pencil a new point, using the hand sharpener in my knapsack. I wanted to make my entry crisp and dark on the page.

There were only two spaces left on the sign-up sheet. The fill-in columns said: NAME _____; NAME OF YOUR ACT _____; TYPE OF ROUTINE _____. I read the first few entries: NAME—Jennifer Newman; NAME OF YOUR ACT—Jennifer's Flips and Folds; TYPE

OF ROUTINE—Gymnastics. Another entry, written toward the bottom of the sheet, was called Now You See It, Now You Don't, a magic routine put on by Lyle Briggs, a boy from Mr. McCurdy's English class.

With my pencil, I wrote in my entry as best I could. NAME—Deirdre Willis; NAME OF YOUR ACT _____. I hadn't thought of a *name* for my act. I didn't really have an *act*. I left that fill-in space blank. Next to TYPE OF ROUTINE, I wrote, Photography Exhibit. I slipped my pencil sharpener back in my knapsack but held on to my pencil.

When I turned around, I was standing face-to-face with Stacy Snead.

"What does Photography Exhibit mean?" Stacy stood with her arms folded.

I said, "It means what I wrote, Photography Exhibit."

Stacy brushed her hair behind one shoulder. "Photography Exhibit *what*?" she asked. "Songs? Music? What are you going to *do*?" I swallowed and folded my arms as tight as Stacy's. "I'm gonna display my pictures. That's my talent."

"I'm sure you think it *is* a talent, but you need to *perform* something."

"Says who?" I got up in Stacy's face. Her head jerked back. She unhooked her arms. I said, "You made that rule up just now."

"And what are you gonna do about it!"

I was breathing so heavy, I could feel my own chest heaving up and down. My clenched fist kept a grip on my pencil. I aimed the pencil point at Stacy's thigh. The point was sharp as a nail.

Real quiet, almost like a whisper, I said, "*Here's* what I'm gonna do." And before Stacy could say another word, I did a slow, steady spin on my heels and printed a new entry in the last column on the sign-up sheet: NAME—Deirdre Willis; NAME OF YOUR ACT—Camera Dee; TYPE OF ROUTINE—Picture Poems!

That night, after dinner, I went straight to my room. I wanted to make my contest exhibit, and I had good news to write to Lorelle.

The letter came first.

> Dear Lorelle,
>
> Get ready to teach me Groove Move! My mom said I could visit during the week of Street Fest. I didn't tell her about Rhonda's fighting and carrying on, but Lorelle, you and me gotta be grown. We're ladies. We need to let Rhonda be, so she can find her own way.
>
> When I visit, I'll be coming on the train to Baltimore's Penn Station. I'll bring my camera and my Jive Five jumping feet!
>
> Guess what? I'm gonna enter my pictures in the Founders' Day Assembly, that school contest I told you about in my last letter. I didn't want to be in it at first. But now I got a strong, quiet feeling inside, makes me want to stand proud and show everybody what I got. When I come, I'll tell you all about it—if you let me do your hair (smile). Wish me luck! See you soon.
>
> Love,
> Dee
>
> P.S. Summer's a short way away. Hey, hey, hey!

I stuck Lorelle's letter in the frame of my dresser mirror so I'd remember to mail it. Then I slid my shoe box full of photos off my closet shelf and spilled the pictures out onto my bed-spread. My favorite shots—the ones I set aside to enter in the Founders' Day Assembly—were the pictures of Dad coming off the train and the photo of Lindsay preparing to teach me lacrosse in our yard. Even though I'd snapped the shot of Linds just a short time ago, to me she looked different in that picture than she did now. Different in a way that was hard to describe. She'd changed since that afternoon on the grass. Less up-jumpy but still full of fire was a good way to put it.

A picture of Mom, sitting on our stoop back at Redmond Avenue, poked out from the bottom of the pile. I'd taken that picture on the day Dad gave me my camera. I studied the photo and saw that my mother was special—tall and tawny, with soul in her eyes, like Daddy always said. I set the picture of Mom near the shots of Dad and Lindsay.

The photos of Lorelle and pictures from the playground at Rosa Parks Public whispered back memories from as long ago as last summer.... *"We call ourselves the Jumpin' Jive Five...."* I smiled, remembering the day me and Lorelle jumped Hell Heel thirty-three times in a row.

In an envelope of newly developed pictures, I found a shot of the doe I'd seen at the end of Scarlet Oak. I looked at the picture for a long minute and saw something in that doe that I hadn't noticed when I spotted her the first time. She was stand-ing alone in a thicket of gnarled trees. But she wasn't the least bit bothered by her aloneness. She stood proud on her four legs, her neck and head held high. It was as if she knew that by taking her place among those trees, on that patch of ground, the woods would be changed. They'd be changed by her just being there—in that moment in my camera's eye. "Wexford Doe, that's your name," I declared with a whisper.

Next to the pictures of Mom, Dad, and Lindsay, I put the

photo of Lorelle and the shot of the Wexford Doe. These were the pictures that meant the most to me—these, I decided, would be my entry.

I sifted through the rest of my pictures and, one by one, stacked them back in their shoe box. When I came to the photos of Stacy Snead, Web's warning—"Blow it up real big.... Stacy is this year's contest judge"—sped through my mind.

Stacy Snead. Hadn't she judged me enough already?

I hissed out a breath, then laid Stacy's picture near the ones I'd picked for my display: Mom, Dad, Lindsay, Lorelle—and Stacy. One look made me shake my head. Stacy Snead had no place in my family picture exhibit. It was as simple as that. I sighed, willing to take my chances by showing up at the Founders' Day Assembly without a picture of Stacy.

I flung Stacy's photo into the shoe box and secured the box lid with a fat rubber band. I didn't know if I was being hard-headed or smart (Mom always said I was a little bit of both), but I was determined to enter the contest with the pictures I liked best.

I pushed the shoe box onto my shelf, buried it behind a pile of winter sweaters, and shoved my cleats on top. I wasn't ever gonna wear those ugly, pinchy cleats again, but Mom told me to keep them to pass on to Lindsay.

I'd bought a piece of poster board, a bottle of glue, and some glitter to make my entry special. On the back of Lorelle's picture, I squirted a zigzag of glue, then carefully pressed the photo in the upper-right-hand corner of the poster board. I positioned the photo of Lindsay on the left and glued the shots of Mom and Dad in the corners below. My picture of the doe belonged in the center. With the glitter, I gave each picture its own sparkly frame.

Before I had a chance to step back and look at my exhibit, Lindsay called me from the stairs. "Yo, Dee! Get down here. It's your turn to push the broom." Lindsay pounded the end of the broom handle on one of the steps. "Dee, the kitchen floor's waiting—on you!"

Holding out my exhibit in front of me, I went to the landing at the top of the stairs. "Linds, check it out—my contest entry."

Lindsay leaned against the banister. She was clutching the broom handle, bristles up. "Where'd you get that deer picture? It looks pretty, Dee."

"I took it—at the dead-end of our street."

"Dee, you did those pictures up *good*."

I walked halfway down the stairs to show Lindsay my pictures up close. "How good?" I asked.

"Camera-Dee-Willis good."

I glanced down over the top of the board. "Winning good?"

"Dee, bet on it. Your pictures got what it takes to walk away with the whole contest."

"Serious, Linds?"

"*Serious,* Dee." Lindsay gestured her broom toward my pictures. "Dee, count on coming home with a prize. The way you sprinkled that shimmery stuff and arranged our family pictures all fancy like that. It's working, Dee. Working to win."

I looked down at my exhibit again. Lindsay was right. My photo display was like nothing else I'd ever seen. I went to the bottom step to give Lindsay a nudge. "How about you finish sweeping the floor for me so I can add more glitter around your picture?"

Lindsay elbowed me back. She held out the broom. "Good try but no go."

12

Two months had passed since I'd come to Wexford Middle School, and now here I was, on the first Friday evening in June, waiting for the Founders' Day Assembly to start.

The auditorium rumbled with whispering parents and restless kids. Mom, Dad, and Lindsay sat in the third row. I sat with the other entrants in a row of folding chairs to the right of the stage. I'd carried my photo exhibit in a large shopping bag that rested at my side. Stacy Snead's seat—a long-legged stool—was up front by the stage. Mr. McCurdy sat next to Stacy. I figured he wanted to be close to the stage to get a good look at the acts. I looked for Web, but didn't see her anywhere.

The Founders' Day Assembly program listed fourteen acts in the order they appeared on the sign-up sheet. My name came last. Lyle Briggs and his magic act were right before me.

Jennifer Newman's gymnastics routine started the show. Her "flips" were more like somersaults, her "folds," back bends. Next came a group of girls who called themselves The Sassy Seventh-Grade Singers. They snapped their fingers and twisted their hips to the music of their own voices. Their rhythm was pretty good.

With each routine, I slid deeper into self-doubt. My entry didn't come with any songs or somersaults. All I had was me and my pictures.

When Lyle Briggs performed his magic act, he wore a top hat and cape. He made a silver dollar disappear. He turned his handkerchief into a bouquet of flowers. He kept the audience clapping for three whole minutes.

After Lyle's applause ended, Stacy skipped to the stage. On her dress, she showed off a purple ribbon with gold letters that said JUDGE. Into the microphone, Stacy said, "We've got one last entry tonight." She turned her eyes in my direction. "Deirdre Willis is going to do something with...pictures."

Slowly, I walked to the stage. My heart thunked a crazy beat inside my chest while my legs turned to macaroni. I wanted to go back to my seat and forget the whole thing. But before I could even think twice about quitting, I heard somebody clapping backstage. I looked over toward the velvety stage curtain and saw Web! She waved and gave me a thumbs-up.

My feet inched toward the edge of the stage. As I lowered my head to introduce myself, the microphone squeaked an awful noise. "My name is Deirdre Wil—" *Squeeeeak*... "And I'm—" *Squeeeeak*... "The name of my routine is—" *Squeeeeeeeak*... My hands trembled, and the flap that was supposed to let sound come out of my throat drew shut. When I looked out at the audience, all I saw was a blur of faces.

Little giggles floated up into the cramped room. Somebody said, "Shush." Someone else whispered, "What on earth...?" Then Web's voice bounced from the curtain: "Keep going, Dee. *Just keep going.*" I closed my eyes. A swirl of confusion clouded my head. My feet, my fingers, my whole body froze.

Mr. McCurdy came up to the stage. On his shirt, he wore a purple satin ribbon like Stacy's. And, like Stacy's, his ribbon said JUDGE. Mr. McCurdy whispered, "Let me lend you a hand." I looked straight into his face, then blinked. His eyes were just as gray as before. But those slate-colored eyes were warm with kindness. "*You're* the judge?" I whispered back.

"The *teacher* judge," he explained. "Stacy's the *student* judge. We'll both be voting on the acts tonight."

Mr. McCurdy adjusted the microphone stand so that the mouthpiece pointed toward my lips. He smiled and patted my shoulder. "It's all yours, Miss Willis."

A snicker and some grumbles seeped from the audience. Stacy yawned. She fanned herself with what looked like a score sheet. I cleared my throat to shake loose the tight, dry skin around my tonsils. "H-e-l-l-o..." I spoke carefully to test the microphone. Instead of squeaks, my voice boomed through the auditorium. "Deirdre Willis is my name. I can't sing that good, and I don't know any magic tricks. But I take some pretty fine pictures. And I like poems by Langston Hughes." As I spoke, my heart jitters floated away. "The name of my act is Picture Poems by Deirdre Willis—Camera Dee Willis. Some people call me Camera Dee because I take so many pictures.

"I took *these* pictures myself. They're portraits of my family, my friend Lorelle, and a doe I spotted in the woods near our house. Wexford Doe, I call her.

"I've picked two Langston Hughes poems to go with my pictures. The first poem, called 'Dreams,' is dedicated to my mom and dad, whose photos I pasted here in the lower corners." I looked out and saw Mom whisper something to Dad. "The poem goes like this.

> *"Hold fast to dreams*
> *For if dreams die*
> *Life is a broken-winged bird*
> *That cannot fly."*

My voice rose clear and strong.

> *"Hold fast to dreams*
> *For when dreams go*
> *Life is a barren field*
> *Frozen with snow."*

The audience got real quiet. They listened to me recite every word. A tiny spark of confidence lit up inside me and quickly grew to a flame. "My next poem by Langston Hughes is called 'Youth,'" I said. "This poem is for my sister, Lindsay, and my friend Lorelle—and for that doe, wherever she is now. Lorelle lives in Baltimore on Redmond Avenue. That's where I used to live, till me and my parents and my sister moved here, to Wexford." I glanced over toward the stage curtain. "Oh—one other thing," I said. "I also want to dedicate this poem to my new friend, Web.

> *"We have tomorrow*
> *Bright before us*
> *Like a flame."*

Offstage, Web was grinning. I nodded to her and kept on with my poem.

"Yesterday, a night-gone thing
A sun-down name.

And dawn today
Broad arch above the road we came.
We march!"

After "We march!" the audience sat still, more silent than the night outside. I thought I'd done something dreadfully wrong, until the smack of Web's clapping hands echoed off the auditorium walls. Lindsay clapped too. So did Mom and Dad. Then a whistle shot up from the back of the auditorium. It was Coach Renner, cheering for *me*. Lyle Briggs waved his top hat. Soon the whole auditorium crackled with praise. Everybody cheered.

Even Stacy Snead clapped for me, but only a little. She was too busy stroking the satin JUDGE ribbon pinned to her dress. She scribbled something on her score sheet and waited for the commotion to die down.

With excitement ballooning inside me, I went back to my folding chair. Stacy and Mr. McCurdy compared their score sheets. They whispered and debated. Then, together, they walked to the stage.

Mr. McCurdy took the microphone from its stand. He held it close to his mouth. "May I have your attention, please." The audience hushed to listen. "This has been quite an evening. We've seen a lot of talent on this stage tonight." Mr. McCurdy nodded toward the group of us entrants fidgeting in our chairs. Stacy wouldn't take her hands off her ribbon.

Mr. McCurdy handed the microphone to Stacy, who, with her hand on her hip, said, "As most of you know, *I* won first place in the Founders' Day Assembly last year with the Snead Cradle, my lacrosse-stick routine. Picking this year's winner was hard." She went on, "Mr. McCurdy and I decided that the prize should go to"—Stacy read from her score sheet; I held my breath—"Lyle Briggs for Now You See It, Now You Don't."

As soon as Stacy read Lyle's name, the audience snapped into applause. Lyle stood up. He marched to the stage, his cape dragging behind him. Stacy presented Lyle with a blue ribbon. She unpinned her JUDGE ribbon and fastened it to his shirt.

I slumped back on my seat to brush off the glitter that had sprinkled from my exhibit to my lap. I was flicking sparkles onto the floor when I heard Stacy announce: "And second place goes to Deirdre Willis for her Picture Poems...." When I looked up, Mr. McCurdy was motioning to me. Stacy was calling my name a second time.

The audience praised me with more clapping. Mr. McCurdy applauded loud as thunder. "Beautiful!" he shouted. "Just beautiful." Then he shook my hand. "Good job," he said. Stacy gave me a red ribbon that I pinned to my own dress.

Lindsay stomped her feet. "Do it, Dee!" she called out. I smiled a smile so big, I thought my cheeks would bust.

After the show, I slid my picture exhibit back into its shopping bag. I met Mom, Dad, and Lindsay by the auditorium EXIT sign. Web was there too. I introduced her to everyone. We joked about the squeaky microphone and laughed all at once.

On the way home, Dad said, "This is a night Bennett Willis will remember for a long time coming."

"Me too," Mom said.

Lindsay joined in: "Me three."

I huffed on the car window to make mist. With my finger, I

drew a flower. Under it I wrote, CAMERA DEE. "Wait till Lorelle sees my red ribbon," I said.

After that, we drove in silence, each settling into our own private thoughts. The moon hung high and full in the blue-black sky. Its pearly, glistening light followed us along the road.